Rendition II

By

JOHN L. BISOL

Rendition II

Published by:
Lulu, Inc.
860 Aviation Parkway, Suite 300
Morrisville, NC 27560

ISBN: 978-0-6151-3560-1

Dedication

This book is dedicated to all the fish in my life:

Carpet

Paws

Fang (Recently Deceased)

Misfit

In addition, my Rodent:

Captain Midnight - *Without his help, this book would have been impossible to write. Truly a great gerbil among mediocre gerbils!*

August 21st, 2006 was a "the Darkest of Days" for my buddy – Captain Midnight. He (apparently) died of a seizure inside his little baking soda box house. He is with the "others" in the Pet Cemetery – out back of the house.

This Page was intentionally - Left Blank!

"Standard DISCLAIMERS"

The Use and Care of Your Book: "Rendition II"

Read only as directed.

During use, do not place or leave the book where it may be damaged by an animal, or exposed to weather.

This book itself does not contain aspirin, but if you are allergic to aspirin do not read - as an adverse reaction may occur.

Keep book away from heated surfaces.

For your protection, do not use if imprinted seal under cap is broken or missing.

Do not use this book with a damaged or broken comb, nor with teeth missing from the blades, as injury may occur.

Before reading, make certain all blades are aligned properly.

Do not place or store where this book can fall or be pulled into a tub or sink.

Do not place in, or drop into, water or other liquid.

Contents are under pressure. Do not puncture or incinerate. Do not store in temperatures above 120 F.

May be irritating to the eyes upon direct contact. In case of eye contact, flush thoroughly with water. If swallowed, drink a glassful of water and call a physician.

Keep this book and all cleaning compounds out of reach of children. (What kind of parent are you, anyway?)

Do not use or mix with other household chemicals such as toilet bowl cleaners, rust removers, acids, or products containing ammonia.

Do not read near open flame. (Exception: STERNO)

For external use only. Consult a doctor for serious burns, paper cuts, or skin disorders.

Do not read this book as a cure for a persistent or chronic cough such as can occur with smoking, asthma, emphysema, or if a cough is accompanied by excessive phlegm (mucus), or if you have a heart disease, high blood pressure, thyroid disease, diabetes, glaucoma, a breathing problem such as emphysema or chronic bronchitis or difficulty in urination due to enlargement of prostate gland, unless directed by a doctor.

A persistent cough may be a sign of a serious condition.

Do not read in cribs, beds, carriages, or playpens.

Objects in this book are closer than they appear.

Readers with kidney or liver disorders should see their physician on a regular basis.

Objects in this book may leap out when book is opened. Do not point this book in the general direction of another person or look directly at the book when opening.

IF YOU CAN READ THIS, YOU ARE TOO CLOSE!

Other Disclaimers:

The author, publisher, editor, distributor, and all parties involved in the creation and distribution of "**I'll Be Watching You**" disclaims any liability of coincidence of similarity of names, places, persons, organizations, locations, quotes or events in this story - with any actual situations, names, places, persons, times, events, locations or organizations. This story is fictional, based on the author's imagination, and the happenstance of seeing two similar buildings. Some historical data was used, but only to make the story readable and as a realistic foundation. Certain phrases and information are included from publicly available documents.

(All I was trying to point out in that story is that silly arguments can be carried to extremes.)

PERMISSIONS, NOTICES - THE USE OF O.P.M. *

I am not as smart as everyone thinks, I do a lot of research, most of which is in public, free sources such as:

Wikipedia, the free-content encyclopedia.
http://en.wikipedia.org/wiki/Main_Page

The *Bible* – any version is fine.

Various Historical Societies in the Keystone State of Pennsylvania.

Hundreds of internet sites on religion, religious orders, and the formation of early religions in America.

Visits to my daughter's house.

* O.P.M. – Other People's Material

Index

Copyright Page/Declaration	*2*
Dedication	*3*
Standard Disclaimers	*5*
Permissions & Notices	*7*
Index	*8*

The Stories Proper

Title	**page**
About The Cover Photo	*9*
Baggers	*10*
Oh Mother, Please!	*16*
Echo...Echo...Echo...Echo...	*19*
Once Upon A Dream	*28*
"I'll Be Watching YOU"	*37*
Familiar	*49*
Standard Curse Page	*63*
Where Are We Now, daddy?	*64*
Deth 2 Squrrelz	*83*
WWW	*96*
Obituary: Rambo (The Cat) Bisol	*106*
Leviticus	*108*
CSI Autopsy Report – Final	*112*

About The Cover Photo

The cover photo shows a wisteria vine slowly girdling a tree. Contrary to popular "romantic" fantasy, wisteria is a parasitic vine, capable of great destruction.

This particular plant appears to be a Chinese wisteria - a deciduous woody vine capable of growing to 70 feet long. Stems can be large (10 inches in diameter) with smooth, tight gray to white bark.

Alternate, pinnately compound leaves are tapered at the tip with wavy edges. Lavender, pink or white flowers are fragrant, very showy, and abundant and occur as dangling clusters. Seed are in a flattened bean-like pod. Chinese wisteria can displace native vegetation and kill trees and shrubs by girdling them. Wisterias have the ability to change the structure of a forest by killing trees and altering the light availability to the forest floor.

These vines can be detrimental to growth of young trees by wrapping tightly around the tree stem. When the tree trunk grows and expands, the vine constricts the flow of water and food. Often the tree is girdled and eventually dies. Winding vines climb by means of tendrils. The tendrils are slim, flexible, and leafless stems that wrap around most anything they contact, such as small branches and twigs. The tendrils are relatively short-lived before withering and losing their grip, but by then the vine is higher in the tree and growing new tendrils for support.

The biggest problem with wisteria is the root system. It can spread over an entire subdivision, pop out in other people's yards and kill their trees, destroy plumbing systems and telecommunications cables.

Note in the cover photo how the tendrils have "reached out" and grasped the adjacent tree, actually bringing it closer to the main vine and in essence, slowly killing it…just like love.

___Baggers___

Dr. *Quasmodus* was a mirthless demon. (Contrary to popular belief, some demons show mirth – even if it is sardonic mirth). He had been assigned the task from "the father of all lies" of developing a way to bring more souls into the nether regions.

For several centuries, he had studied the concept of "free will" and at last, he felt he had found a loophole.

He had observed that in moments of extreme anxiety (or horror), as the subject faced death, they often did NOT pray to the LORD – they did not pray to anyone because their primal instinct overruled reason. It was, in those microseconds, that the soul was easily conscripted by a "Bagger."

A "Bagger" is the demon opposite of an angel. They are soul "stealers" – rather than guiding. They simply take souls to the nether regions without permission from the owner.

For example, there was the loathsome *Reptilius Virus.* As an evil spirit, he had no redeeming qualities. He was so bereft of anything that he was doomed to be a "Bagger" for all eternity.

Reptilius' specialty was sudden death by accident. It did not matter if by plane, train, car, or electric shock, he "Bagged" the souls at the instant of death. Sometimes he was a little "too quick" and the body was doomed to a vegetative state, (kept alive by machines and the hope of loved ones).

Reptilius often sniggered at the reprimands he would receive. (Even in death, there are Rules of Engagement).

"So I'm a spirit assassin. Send me to hell," he would say as he skulked into the eternal shadows. That attitude was one reason why he was relegated to filth and deprivation.

As things unfolded, *Dr. Quasmodus* was asked to provide a demonstration of the theory of "Free Will Lapse."

"The END TIME is approaching." The liar had told him during their latest meeting.

"I need to have a demonstration of your theory. Nothing too spectacular, but enough so I can have some hard data, numbers if you will, to make a projection of what I can expect."

Dr. Quasmodus knew it was all lies (of course), but he was sick and tired of having to observe, he wanted to lead.

"Take *Reptilius* with you – train a cadre of 'Baggers' and let the test begin," the liar turned quickly, disappearing before there could be any questions.

"So, does that mean I have a day or an eon?" *Dr. Quasmodus* said into the void. No sound came forth.

"*Reptilius!*" he roared, "Where are you? *Reptilius!*" ...

...The rain slanted across the parking lot. The low, scudding clouds were being gusted across the sky.

"Now Lilly, you sit here, I'm going to get some bread. I'll be right back." Arthur Cantwin looked across at his elderly mother. She was "double-strapped" into the front passenger seat. The oxygen mask hissed incessantly and the only way Arthur knew she was alive was by the fog on the mask that formed as she exhaled.

She sat rigid and stared straight ahead, never acknowledging Arthur as he slammed the door shut.

Reptilius Virus reached over the seat back and "Bagged" Lilly's soul. She did not flinch, but no moisture formed on the mask…

…"Where is that vermin *Reptilius?*" *Dr. Quasmodus* muttered as he paced the floor of the "Ready-Set-GO!" Mart.

"Hey! It's me, doc," *Reptilius* held a squirming sack in one hand.

"Is that what I think it is?" *Dr. Quasmodus* asked angrily.

"Yeh, well you see, sometimes it doesn't know it's dead." *Reptilius* replied as he moved his hand over the sack and squeezed until the movement stopped. "OK, NOW - it's dead."

"Are your 'Baggers' ready?" *Dr. Quasmodus* asked in resignation.

"Yes, yes they are," Reptilius, replied as he nervously glanced around for his legion. He hoped that none of them was prematurely "Bagging." His fears were realized when he heard a scream from aisle 7B – Housewares & Sundries.

"Hey, don't look at me; it must be a rogue agent." *Reptilius* cowed from *Dr. Quasmodus'* angry glare. "I'll just see who it is."

"Be ready when I call you, and no more shenanigans!" *Dr. Quasmodus* flicked a pain dart into *Reptilius'* backside.

Dr. Quasmodus surveyed the "Ready-Set-GO!" Mart. It was not what he had hoped for, but for him, life was, well life was hell.

The store had 24 aisles for shoppers and it was crowded, despite the rain. There was a crowd gathering around the woman who had died unexpectedly, in aisle 7B. Someone was kneeling next to her attempting to feel for some sign of life.

"Well," *Dr. Quasmodus* said, "It's show and tell time! Lightning!" There was a bright flash of lightning and a sharp crack of thunder, the store lights went out. At the same moment, the security shutters rolled down over the windows and the outside doors locked, the robbery gates slowly descending into place. Few patrons noticed this because they were still reacting to the darkness. A voice came on the loudspeaker.

"Attention 'Ready-Set-GO!' Mart Shoppers. The store has experienced a temporary loss of power. In a moment, our back-up generator will restore all electrical functions and store personnel will be ready to serve you. In the next few seconds, until power is restored, please continue to shop."

"Flame!" *Dr. Quasmodus* said. A sheet of orange flame burst out from under the walls of the store.

Dr. Quasmodus moved to the manager's office. There was a young man seated in a chair, overlooking the store through the two-way mirrored glass, in disbelief.

Dr. Quasmodus flicked him in the neck with his finger and he died. Smoke began to billow from the rear storerooms. The customers began to move to the front of the building, only to see the hordes of "Baggers" blocking the doors. Panic had arrived.

Dr. Quasmodus picked up the microphone from the dead boy's hand, adjusted it slightly, and said (in his best manager's voice), "All 'Baggers' up front" – and the hordes of "Baggers" marched the crowd forward.

Oh Mother, Please!

"Mother May I?" was the game they had played for almost fifty years. Theodore Winnot finally was able to watch his mother die. There was a time, when he was in his mid 30s, that Theodore thought his mother would outlive him. She was simply a demanding, nagging "bitch." No matter what, she had managed to insert herself in his life and control and destroy everything he wanted. She was like "loosestrife," growing everywhere and killing all she came across, yet appearing to be the most beautiful flower on earth.

She had ruined two engagements, destroyed all his social life, and sucked him dry financially, demanding one thing or another.

Finally, he could take no more, and on his fifty-first birthday, he had left her. He moved across town to a new apartment and left her alone in the house. Two days later she was dead – suicide, of course. The note they found expressed her anguish over his leaving her and how her life was over..."Blah! Blah! Blah! Blah! Blah!" (All carefully created to make him look bad.)

Theodore knew the truth. He had come over that suicide night, earlier. She told him what she was going to do. She told him all about the "overdose" and how she would call her "real friends" to come to save her once she had taken the pills. She waved the bottle in his face and left the room in a huff. Theodore looked at the bottle on the nightstand. He picked it up and rolled it in his hand. Without hesitation, he opened it, dumped the sleeping pills into his pocket, and poured twelve cyanide pills in their stead.

She was still ranting when she returned. "You'll be humiliated," she said. "No one will love you after they find out you broke your mother's heart. No One!"

"Go ahead and do it, but don't forget to take enough to make it look good," Theodore said as he left.

He drove to McGinty's and waited to be contacted.

Within an hour, a dour looking uniformed Police Officer came in and scanned the crowd. Someone pointed to Theodore.

"Are you Theodore Winnot?" the officer asked as he approached Theodore.

"Yes I am. What is it?" Theodore feigned dismay.

"We received a 'Medic-Distress' call from your mother's pager. She's dead Mr. Winnot, suicide."

Now, two days later, he had returned to his new apartment, with his mother's ashes in a simple grey urn. There was no ceremony, Theodore saw to that. He was not going to allow his mother a last chance to steal the show. Simple cremation, he had explained to the undertaker, simple cremation. He held the remains in his hand. This was his time for "payback."

A swirl of black dust curled up out of the opening as Theodore popped the lid of the urn. (Was mother rising from the dead?) He looked inside. The remains appeared to be something like cement dust. Theodore moved to the bathroom. He unzipped his fly and urinated into the urn. There was a hissing sound as the stream hit "paydirt." The urn became heavy and warm. Theodore was relieved.

"What's that mother?" he said as he looked at the eddying foam near the mouth of the urn.

"You want to be shaken – not stirred?" Theodore replaced the lid tightly and shook the urn violently.

"You're welcome, mother. You must be tired after your long trip. How about a nice swirly bath? Oh mother, you will love it. The water is so refreshing and blue."

Theodore stood over the toilet and raised the seat. He removed the lid from the urn and tilted the urn slightly. The dark contents slopped into the water, each blob spreading as it sank.

"There, there –almost done, quick rinse," he put the urn under the sink spout and let some water flow into it.

"Now a final, cleansing, twist or two," he rotated the urn several times and then turned it upside down over the toilet – a last few blobs fell out.

"Swirly bath time!" Theodore flushed the toilet. "Oh! Look at you go, mother!"

The toilet gurgled noisily. Theodore waited until the water settled. He sighed heavily.

"Now I can take a nice, peaceful 'dump'," he said as he dropped his pants and sat down.

Echo...Echo...Echo...Echo...

**"...Echo; the nymph who was spurned by Narcissus and pined away until only her voice remained..."**

i.

A hot sun beat down on the bone-dry soil. Martin Finch tried not to look out across the dusty plain; the glare hurt his eyes too much. He kicked a bit of the soil and a small cloud swirled in the heated air.

"If we don't find a way in, we'll have to drill a borehole," Nugent said.

"Boreholes cost money," Martin grunted. "We could pay some locals to dig a pit and then cut our way in."

"Nasty job in this heat. I should have joined the Arctic team." Nugent made an entry in his logbook. "I'll set Kuolous on it right away. What do you think – ten or fifteen feet?"

"I'm not sure when they'll get through the top layer; let's say fifteen to be certain."

Finally, Martin lifted his eyes and gazed as best he could across the parched, dome-shaped field. Heat waves caused the edges of the field to shimmer and disappear. A solitary locust hopped across his shoe and landed on a burned stalk of grass. For a moment, it balanced itself and then, slowly swung under the stalk as if to seek some shelter from the sun.

"Nasty grant, this geology thing. Let's go back to camp and see what's what."

The two men made dusty footprints in the dirt; soon, a hot wind filled them in…

The empty magma chamber had been only recently discovered. Two students from the London University had been seismic probing a small island off the coast of Greece when they had come across the anomaly. Naturally, Doctor Carter had been notified and he quickly dispatched a spelunking team in the hopes of entering the chamber and documenting it.

The team had spent almost a week on the site trying to find a way in that would not compromise the delicate structures they expected to find in the main chamber.

They hired the laborers, locals, who did not seem to mind the heat. The men joked as they dug a funnel shaped pit. The dirt had to be carted a distance away because it kept falling back into the hole.

Finally, after four days they had made something akin to an ant lion structure. Just after noon, the workers struck rock and began to hoot and holler. They bridged the hole with planks and mounted a derrick in the middle. A rock drill was engaged, and by early afternoon, a swirling cloud of stone chips, dust, and ash was rising from the pit.

Just before sunset, there was a loud report and a crack! The magma chamber had been breached. The workers pulled the drill apparatus from the pit and in the shimmering twilight, they headed back to their homes in their filthy, rusted trucks.

No sooner had the workers left, then a set of headlights appeared on the edge of the field, belonging to a red Land Rover driven by Robert Cranston. Cranston was the leader of the spelunkers. He had a nasty habit of pestering the geologists everyday as to their progress, and when he might enter the chamber.

"Here comes God's gift to the cave world," Nugent said as he waved his tin drinking cup in the direction of the truck pulling a dust cloud behind it.

In a scattering of stones and the truck skidded to a stop.

"Go home, not tonight," Martin gestured.

Cranston was already out of the truck. "How close are we?" He said as he slapped the dust off his shirt.

"Well, they broke through, but we should wait until tomorrow for venting of gases and such," Nugent stated.

"I'll have a look then. Bring my gear over to the hole," Cranston swung himself back into the truck.

"Mind you, now, no torches or flames near the opening. We haven't had time to check for anything coming out. Could be poisonous, could be flammable, all sorts of bloody awful stuff possible," Martin yelled as he stood up.

Cranston simply gave thumbs up and drove over to the pit. They watched as he began to carry rope and equipment from the truck into the pit.

"Always in such a bloody rush. I hope he doesn't fall in. I'll call the rest of the team in the morning." Nugent stretched and motioned to the sky.

"Good night for sleeping. Some progress today."

"Yes. Good night," Martin said as he moved towards his tent.

At the pit, Cranston was busily placing his equipment. He didn't mind the glooming darkness. He worked quickly with only his miner's lamp for light. Several times as he neared the opening he thought he could hear 'something' inside the chamber, but he dismissed it as escaping gases, or rock falls.

ii.

Finally, he saw the lights in the tents go out. They must have gone to sleep, he thought.

Cranston put on his rappelling harness. He brought one end of his rope to the Land Rover and hooked on to the truck.

"Now we'll have a look inside a bit." He said as he deftly walked to the opening.

He peered over the edge. (Nothing, of course, only blackness.) He sniffed at the air. No fumes that he could detect. (What the hell, he would go in about ten feet and have a look around).

With a short hop, he launched himself into the void. Carefully he played out some rope until he was hanging in the vast, black oblivion. His lamp was not strong enough to illuminate any of the walls of the chamber. If he looked directly up, he was able to see that the rock face was smooth, black obsidian rock. There was no way to tell how far down to the bottom. Robert Cranston let out another length of line. The marks on the rope showed him to be fifty feet into the chamber. More line was let…one hundred feet….one hundred and fifty…two hundred feet…two hundred and fifty… (The small opening was now gone, mixed black with the night sky)…three hundred…he thought he could begin to see the bottom. He guessed there was another ten or fifteen feet to go, but he was literally, at the end of his rope. No matter, he would drop to the floor, spend the night and they would have to get him out tomorrow. He hoped the floor wasn't rough. He let go.

For a second he thought he wasn't going to stop, but then he realized that the floor was perfectly smooth and when he landed, he simply slid for a distance. Now he was away from the rope. It was beyond the reach of his lamp. He wished he could use a flare for light, but that might have consequences.

As he sat on the floor, he became aware of a subtle sound. It was rhythmic and seemed to come from far away. He realized that within the spherical chamber – he could only imagine its size; he was hearing the echo of his own breathing!

His miner's lamp shown only a small cone of comfort around him. Everything was sterile on the floor; it simply was black and shiny, like some horrifying cat's eye. This was an uncomfortable fix! He was stuck here until the morning.

Still he heard his own breathing, distant yet close. He stood up and started to walk back in the direction from where he thought he had slid. The chamber wasn't unusually cold or warm, it seemed just right. There was no wind or air movement, yet Robert thought he detected a hint of lilac in the air. He might have accepted sulfur, but lilac was strange indeed. A few steps ahead of him he began to discern something that looked like a rock outcropping. As he neared, he could see it was a shelf in the middle of black nothing, surrounded by space.

Cranston sat down. The echoes of his movement returned in a few seconds. He could hear the clink of his harness and the distinct "plop" as he sat down, and always, his own breathing.

"Time to sleep," he muttered.

"SSSSSsssslllleeepppp," returned from somewhere.

He lay on the shelf and waited for the sounds to die down. He slept. He dreamed of a verdant field of flowers. There was laughter around him, but he could see no one…or was that wisp of white in the corner of his eye…a fleeting glance of something? He called out in his dream, "Who's there?" However, all he got back was the same echoing question, "…there?"

After a short time, he awoke and all was silent, but he began to hear giggles and laughter, as if someone were observing him from afar and found it humorous that he was so confused. "Show yourself!" he shouted in his dreams. "…Self!" came back from somewhere behind him.

He fell back asleep. The dream returned and went on for a long time and Robert became quite agitated. Several times, he thought he saw a young girl running beside him, but each time he stopped to look, she vanished.

Finally, he pretended not to see her and when he was certain she was behind him he stopped short and grabbed her as she darted by. He felt a tug, but she was gone. Cranston awoke with a start.

He didn't bother to switch on his lamp but he sat upright and cocked his hand to his ear to hear better.

There were echoes coming, but they were of his <u>own</u> thoughts, alive with sound! He could hear his <u>own</u> heart throbbing. He could hear his pulse, but most of all he could hear himself screaming to "STOP IT! STOP IT!" and always the laughter was nowhere but everywhere.

iii.

"Bloody Hell!" Martin exclaimed as he opened his tent flap and saw the Land Rover still on the edge of the pit.

An orange red sunrise bathed the scene in a macabre tone of death.

"Nugent, Nugent! That fool Cranston must have fallen into the pit! Get the others, hurry!" Martin ran for the excavation.

When he arrived, all he saw was the rope over the edge, into the void. The morning sun was no match for the eternal blackness. He saw the familiar cloud of dust rising as the others in the party approached, all clamoring for information on what was happening.

The oppressive heat was quick to overtake them…

iv.

...The laborers moved boxes off the flatbed and placed them on filthy cargo netting...

Five of them had descended into the magma chamber looking for Cranston. Martin could not help but remember the image he had last seen when his lamp had illuminated the remains of Robert Cranston.

Cranston was found sitting perfectly still, on a rock shelf at the bottom of the chamber, one hand cocked behind his right ear, as if he were listening for something. Yet Cranston was quite dead. His body was rigid and although his skin felt almost desiccated; Cranston was made of stone! The miner's lamp on his helmet was dim and fading, flickering in its last efforts.

What made the scene worse was that everyone could distinctly hear someone's voice, echoing and saying over and over again....

"Please, don't hold me...Please, don't hold me... Please, don't hold me...Please, don't hold me... Please, don't hold me...Please, don't hold me..."

They had left him there. No one had moved him. It was something Nugent had said that caused them to leave him.

"We must not disturb the 'confinement' of the tomb. Bloody bad curse if we do..."

...The sun was unusually strong. Martin stopped long enough to hear a tour guide speaking to a group of children.

"…From that time forth, Echo lived in caves till at last all her flesh shrank away. Her bones were changed into rocks and there was nothing left of her but her voice. With that, she is still ready to reply to any one who calls her, and keeps up her old habit of having the last word…."

Author's Preface:

I do not want to disrespect "The Mouse", but one of the scariest songs in the universe is in "*Sleeping Beauty*" *(the <u>cartoon version</u>, not the ballet).* We have all heard the driving melody from Tchaikovsky; but the lyrics by Sammy Fain and Jack Lawrence are more than just a happy lilt. Consider the following....

<u>*Once Upon A Dream*</u>

"I know you..."

The first time Tom Meager had the dream, he thought it was funny. He had been working on a lengthy report concerning Asian Sales when he simply fell asleep at his computer. He was not certain if the light was from the computer screen or something else, but a rusty red glow diffused his vision.

Meager was going to be married in seven weeks to Jen Russet. Jen was a cute girl he had met from Accounting. They had been going together for almost a year when she suddenly asked him to marry her. At first, Tom was annoyed, he liked to be in charge of things, but somehow he had said yes, and the next thing he knew, Jen was planning the whole thing.

In his dream, he saw a yellow phantom emerge from the blood red mist. First, it seemed to be a swirling mass of light, but it evolved into a naked female form. She raced towards him and before he knew it, she was hugging and squeezing him. Her face was changing rapidly from one of a girlfriend he knew in high school, to Jen, to some other girl he knew in Junior High, to some woman in the bank, and on and on.

He could hardly catch his breath. The form leapt at him. She began kissing him everywhere he could imagine, and then they were tumbling together in an embrace through some sort of tunnel, until Tom saw that they were approaching a wall or barrier. When they hit it, pain raced through his body and he jumped. He fell out of his chair and landed heavily on the floor. He ached everywhere and for a few minutes, he lay on the floor, barely breathing.

"...I walked with you once upon a dream..."

"What happened to you?" Arthur Greeves asked as Tom walked into the office.

"Why, do I look that bad?" Meager said as he dropped into a chair.

"You look like you went ten rounds with a female Primo Canera, you old rooster," Arthur tapped Tom on the shoulder.

"Take it easy! It's nothing, I must be getting the flu, or some other bug. That's all." Meager growled.

"...I know you..."

She came back exactly on the night of the new moon, one month later. As before, it was a bone wrenching experience culminated by pain and agony as Tom Meager found himself tossed onto the bedroom floor. Bruised and battered he struggled to shower and dress himself. Some of the cuts on his face were still bleeding when he walked into his office.

"Have you been in a fight, Tom?" the receptionist asked.

"No, no fight. I just slipped on the stairs to my apartment." He said as he turned his head to one side to avoid her stare.

"...The gleam in your eyes is so familiar a gleam..."

The third nightly visit was the worst yet. Meager felt he was being tossed around and thrown off a cliff at the same time. The vision had an insatiable sexual appetite. Whatever it was seemed to squeeze the life out of him, and in the end, he lay battered on the floor, exhausted and bruised.

Tom thought he was possessed of a vampire, or at least in bed with one. There were no fang marks on his neck, not even a telltale "hickey" the next day.

This time Arthur was not so kind.

"You look trashed, Tom." He said.

Arthur closed the office door behind himself.

"I know you're getting married in a few days, but this is something serious. Whatever is after you, whatever is beating you up; well, I think it's unholy. I want you to meet a friend of mine, Dr. Qualia. I took a couple of his courses in college and he gave me some insight into a lot of things."

"I don't need a doctor," Meager protested.

"He isn't your run of the mill pill pusher. He is good, and he knows his stuff. Tomorrow, nine AM, be there," Greeves handed Tom a "Post-it" note with the information.

"Oh Crap!" Meager said.

"Be there or don't come to work anymore here. You look like death warmed over. Christ! You're scaring Buzzy the midget in the mailroom. You won't be sorry." Arthur said as he left.

"...Yes, I know it's true that visions are seldom all they seem..."

Tom Meager found himself outside the office of Dr. Lucius Qualia. The lettering on the door had the educator's name and a dozen initials beside the PhD. It was the title of "Demonology Department Head" that bothered Meager the most.

The office was predictably gloomy with the blinds half closed and a clutter of textbooks bursting every horizontal surface.

"So you're Tom Meager," Dr. Qualia said as he extended a hand.

For a moment, Tom thought he was looking into the eyes of Colonel Sanders – the white suit and goatee.

"Yes, yes, I am," he said.

"Come in and tell me, when the visitations began..."

Tom Meager spent the next hour trying to be as truthful as possible without sounding ridiculous. He told Dr. Qualia just about everything but he left the sexual overtones out.

"From your description I would say you have been in consort with a succubus."

Dr. Qualia rose from his chair and went to the bookcase. He scanned the titles and then picked out one source. The book cover was somewhat ragged, leather, and cracked. Qualia fingered through several pages.

"Ah, Yes, here is the reference," he placed the book on the desk and turned it towards Meager.

"…The succubus is often said to have originated from a single demon - Lilith. According to ancient Semitic legend, Lilith was the first wife of Adam, made from filth before the creation of Eve. She went off to mate with fallen angels who spawned a great family of demons upon her. These are the *lilim*, who seduce and weaken men in the silence of the night."

"I've never heard of such a thing," Meager said", this is not mentioned in my Bible or Religion."

"There are many *unpublished* books in each and every religion. Things that were not meant to be known to the common person were conveniently left out by the 'Founding Fathers' of the mainstream religions. Call it a way to get their viewpoint across without any questions."

Qualia closed the book. "Lilith, aside from a stray reference comparing her to a 'screech owl', does not appear in the Bible itself. It is in Rabbinic Midrash that we find the full delineation of Lilith."

"How can this be? Are you saying this is a real creature?" protested Meager.

"As real as your angels, and Holy Spirit." Qualia looked out the window as if he had seen someone looking in. "This is the true question - If woman was created from Adam, after his initial creation, than what happened to the female created at first?"

Qualia stood and moved to the window to look out.

"The answer, according to the Midrash, was that she was Lilith; created <u>with</u> Adam, she refused to comply with Adam's demand that she submit herself to him, and in the end fled from him by using the Ineffable Name," he continued.

"What is the Ineffable Name?" Meager was becoming confused, this sounded like mystical mumbo-jumbo.

"To say that something is 'ineffable' means that it cannot or should not be spoken," Qualia explained. "The Tetragrammaton or Yahweh (by orthodox Jewish tradition) is such a Name. We have our modern examples, names of various villains in works of fiction, Lord Voldemort in the *Harry Potter* books or the 'Dark One' in *The Wheel of Time* sequence. Those are names, which should not be spoken, lest the evil descend upon the speaker. To say the Name, invokes the evil."

"You said Lilith fled, so why is she of any concern to any of us?"

"Things are not always so simple where evil is concerned." Qualia moved back to his desk and sat down. He placed a small wooden crucifix on his desk blotter.

"Adam then complained to God about his loneliness, and the creation of Eve followed, together with the 'Fall from Grace' and the Expulsion from Eden. Adam, blaming all this on Eve, separated from her, and for a time he reunited with Lilith, before finally returning to Eve." Qualia began to write something on his notepad while he spoke.

"Lilith bore Adam a number of children in this dark interval, which became the demons we know today. After Adam's reconciliation with Eve, Lilith assumed the Queenship of the Demons; in some versions, she is the consort of Samael, in others, she remains unpartnered."

"Samael? You lost me there." Meager cut in.

"Yes, of course, Samael is an important figure in Talmudic and post-Talmudic lore, a figure who is accuser, seducer, and destroyer. Legends referring to Satan refer equally to him, such that Samael is often taken to be the true or angelic name of the Devil, as opposed to the epithet, Lucifer, which is based on a misapprehension of a verse against the King of Tyre, or the job title, Satan (Adversary). Samael cannot be simply identified with Satan, since in the Books of Enoch, Satan's angelic name is confirmed to be Satanail or Satanael."

Meager could not absorb all he was hearing. He knew it was not a "good thing" and that scared him.

Dr. Qualia continued. "Samael is etymologized as 'Venom of God,' since he is sometimes identified with the Angel of death. In Jewish lore, he is said to be chief ruler of the seventh Heaven, one of the 7 regents of the world served by 2 million angels; on the other hand, St. John speaks of him in Revelations as the 'great serpent with 12 wings that draws after him, in his fall, the solar system.' Yalkut I, 110 of the Talmud speaks of Samael as Esau's guardian angel. In Sotah 10b, Samael is Edom's guardian angel, and in the Sayings of Rabbi

Eliezer, he is charged with being the one who tempted Eve, then seduced and impregnated her with Cain. Samael is also identified as being the angelic antagonist that wrestled Jacob at Esau. In The Holy Kabbalah, Samael is described as the "severity of God" and is listed as fifth of the archangels of the world of Briah. According to Zoharistic cabala, also among Samael's mates were Eisheth Zenunium, Naamah, and Agrat bat Mahlat - all angels of prostitution. Samael is also perhaps the true personification of Wrath, rather than Satan, seeing as how Samael is also sometimes associated with Asmodeus, the demon of lust and wrath, and Satan is considered a juridical adversary, directed by God."

"So what do I do about this?" Meager asked after the sermon.

"My advice to you is to fill your life with more things Holy. You need a sense of permanency in your life. Sometimes marriage helps, not from a sexual perspective, but that the bonds of marriage are strong and can resist the influence of a succubus." Dr. Qualia rubbed his forehead.

"There is one more danger with marriage," He said. "One more danger..."

"...But if I know you, I know what you'll do.
You'll love me at once the way you did once upon a dream."

The wedding had been beautiful. True to Dr. Qualia's prediction, Lilith had not returned after Tom's marriage. For the first month, everything was wonderful. Then, Jen announced she was three months' pregnant, and Meager entered a new frame of anxiety. Dr.

Qualia had provided him with a detailed explanation of what this succubus, Lilith, was capable of….

"…As long as a child is conceived <u>after</u> the marriage is consummated, there is only one harm she can perform. However, should a child be conceived out of wedlock, then there are a range of things that have been attributed to her wrath, miscarriage being the mildest, all the way to a stillborn child. Please be careful, Mr. Meager…"

Tom was more than a nervous wreck for the remaining six months, whereas Jen attributed his anxiety to "sympathy" and "caring".

However, the pregnancy was remarkably easy on both of them and Thomas Meager Junior was born on the 15th of August. The infant seemed robust and in good health. The hospital stay was two days and mother and child went home with only the happiest thoughts.

Their first night at home seemed quiet enough, but Tom had a gnawing in his soul that would not let him rest. He followed Jen and Tom Jr. to the crib.

"Oh Tom, we'll be the best parents ever!" Jen said as she held the infant close. She laid the small child on a lace pillow and they both gazed at the peaceful smile on Tom Jr's. sleeping face.

Meager could only shudder. He remembered the rest of what Dr. Qualia had told him.

"...As Queen of the Demons, Lilith, out of jealousy, kills infants in their cribs; this was the folk explanation of SIDS."

"I'll Be Watching YOU"

for: Andrea and James – 15 July 2004

Sometimes a vacation can be a real "Godsend". This past summer was no exception. We were driving along a picturesque county road not to far from the Keystone State capital when I saw the "twins" – two almost identical churches on opposite sides of the road, facing each other.

At first, I had to remember to drive, lest the energetic pick-up truck behind forced me into an off-road adventure. Eventually there was time to stop, turn around, and come back to stare at the way these two buildings stood.

They were made of the same materials and were architecturally "fraternal twins." Small nuances in the doors and windows were the only distinguishing marks. One was the **Christ United Churches of Christ** and the other the **Christ Evangelical Church of Christ**. They were equally placed on their respective lots, and as near, as I could determine, they were in a straight line from the center of one set of doors to the center of the opposite set of doors. Since we were staying in a hotel not too far from these churches I knew I would pass them everyday for the next week.

Having said that, it was one our first return trip at night that the story became a little less clear. We were returning to the hotel around midnight, after a fine party with friends, and as we cleared the crest of the small knoll, we could see the shadow outlines of the two churches. There was one stark difference, however, one church was brightly lit from the interior and shown a kaleidoscope of colors in the evening haze, while the other church was dark and appeared to be nothing more than a blacker outline on the road.

The next day I went to the local historical society and began some research. The volunteer on duty was a severe looking woman (in her mid 40s, I would guess). She wasn't particularly helpful, but she was rude and curt. The brief article she handed me to "read and return" was simply a statement of fact:

"The present day Christ Evangelical Church of Christ was first known as the Christ Reformed Church of Christ and was originally founded as a Union Church of Christ on October 22, 1828, holding joint services with the Lutherans. The worship services were held in the same building, located directly across the street 'on the eastern side of the great road called, 'Fort Dale Road', Clark Township in the county of Sheldon.

It was under the ministry of its ninth pastor; Rev. D.R. Slagemeister (1902-1911), that the Reformed congregations began plans to dissolve. Marked by several changes, including the discontinuation of Austrian singing in the worship services and the formation of a Sunday School, it was during his pastorate that the agreement to separate from the Union Church was signed. In 1911, each congregation decided to build its own sanctuary.

From a newspaper clipping:

"Completed in the summer of 1913, the new church building, Christ United Churches of Christ, was dedicated June 3 of that same year. The new sanctuary and educational facilities were built in 1956. From the beginning, the members of both Churches have been called to be God's witness in this community. Their mission remains the same: "to help all men and women love and serve Jesus Christ.""

I knew immediately what an "organic pile" that article was, but I also knew I wasn't going to get the truth from the woman at the Historical Society. I thanked her for he time and effort and left the building, all the time under her watchful eye.

It happened that the next day I stopped at the supermarket to pick up a few items for that night's dinner. I was immersed in the aisles, trying to figure out the store layout when two men approached.

One was a store employee by witness of his apron and blue uniform, while the other was a somber, medium build elderly man.

"Excuse me sir, but I understand from my friends that you are interested in the history of the churches," the older one said. The store clerk seemed to fade away as if he were never there.

"Well, I was curious about the way things were built and so on, but the historical society really didn't have much to build on. I'm Mike Harlan," I said extending my hand.

"Leon Pfalz, local historian and keeper of things past and present," he said as he shook my hand.

"It's by design there isn't much about the two churches in the historical society. Most church members value their privacy and tend to feel that what happened was their business and it is not meant to be shared with outsiders." He continued.

"Well, I wasn't trying to pry. I'm just naturally curious about the way things are. I felt the churches were built that way either by accident or because of some unique happenstance. It's not often you see identical buildings and opposing cemeteries on any road." I almost started to sound defensive.

"Well, you are right about the happenstance. Do you have a few minutes? There's a coffee shop in the store and I can fill you in on all you need to know."

"Sure, I have time." The hook was that my own curiosity was getting the better of my judgment. Maybe the historical society volunteer was some sort of "social spy" for the town. OK, I was fantasizing.

We sat near the windows of the little store shop. I could tell Mr. Pfalz was a self-assured, well-educated person. He seemed unimpressed when two people in an adjoining table abruptly stood up and left as we approached. They acted as if they had been "chased away" by his presence. I wondered if Pfalz was a police officer or some other public official.

"Let me begin by saying that I am the elder appointed communicator for the Christ United Churches of Christ. The original congregation. The Austrian Reformed Church established in 16th-century Austria under the influence of Ulrich Zwingli and John Calvin.

When William Penn offered an invitation to his colony in the new world, thousands of persecuted Austrian Reformers immigrated to Pennsylvania. They brought with them their Austrian Bibles, hymnbooks, and catechisms, determined to preserve their faith in the new world.

As you may have found out some townspeople call us the 'dark' church, but that is from their ignorance of the facts." He explained.

I hadn't heard about the "dark" church from anyone local, but it was my impression the night I drove by the two buildings.

"It is their defiance of the way which causes them to be jubilant and flaunt the light," he added somberly.

"As you know we once shared the same meetinghouse, but we grew apart over certain differences in adoration. There were newcomers who did not appreciate what had been done before and the group split into two denominations.

Those who were critical of our denomination pointed to several things. First, of course, the Church people, the Austrian Reformed people saw emotional and lively worship as altogether unfitting. Worship for us had to be formal and had to be liturgical. Even singing was to be done on a level that was both respectful and non-joyous.

Then there was problems arising with the testimonies of the newcomers. There was a lot of talk in the neighborhood about the testimonies that were given in those days. My grandmother remembered hearing a Mr. Jonas Balk give his Testimony. She said that Jonas Balk had had an alcohol problem in his lifetime and had; because of the alcohol problem, he frittered away his farm. Everyone knew this in the community, no one talked about it in public, (because, after all, alcoholism was a private matter). My grandmother said she would never forget him standing up in prayer meeting or whatever and saying; *"I have been drinking since the sun came up today."* She wasn't certain if he was drunk at the time, or sober and repentant. It was just too much public information.

People who were of different persuasions thought that this enthusiasm, this 'getting happy,' 'getting blessed,' jumping and shouting, praising the Lord aloud was necessary, but we knew they were not in order. There was a lot of two-way criticism of that opinion. Once, my parents took me to one of these so-called, 'happy meetings' after the groups had split, I was determined to learn all I could about the goings on. I was scared. During the meeting, a sister jumped up and let out a shriek. My mother said I crept under her skirts. I was scared, I did not know what was going on, but she was, I am sure, very sincere and was praising her Lord.

I can also remember hearing my grandfather explain the different times and places he gave his own testimony. He cursed one man who stood and said, "*Oh, I am happy that I'm here!*" That 'outburst' of emotionalism was something that religions that are more staid could not stand." Pfalz paused for effect to judge my reaction.

"You are a religious man, Mr. Harlan, because these things have no meaning for the non-believer," he said.

"I'm a Roman Catholic," I answered.

"Ah! A Papist Sprinkler!" he said with glee. "I am a Dunken, you know, not a Papist Sprinkler as you profess to be."

"I don't know what a Dunken is," I replied, not knowing where the conversation was headed.

"'Dunken' began as a critical term, a derogatory term, just like the term 'Quaker'. We were called a 'Dunker' or 'Dunkens' by the people who were against us because we dunked people in water. For example, the Church of the New Brotherhood are Dunkens. Our official name was Austrian Baptist Brotherhood Church until 1908 when it was officially changed from Austrian Baptist Brotherhood Church to Church of the Brotherhood. Now there is still an old Austrian Baptist Brotherhood Church, what we call 'Old Order Dunkens', which are very, very plain people. The River Brotherhood are another group. While they are called Brotherhood in Christ today in this part of the country, having a congregation here in the Valley and congregations over in Solderton and Riverdale in Lamb County, they came from an immersionist movement within the Walton Church in Cheshire County in the 1770's. Therefore, Brotherhood in Christ are Waltons who wanted to baptize by immersion."

"How does all this tie in to the two churches?" I asked (not wanting to continue to undergo an immersion-conversion myself).

"There were problems with the newcomers, the outside groups coming to the valley in the early 1900s. I understand one group approached our Dunken bishops and said, 'Baptize us by immersion, but then we want to go back and stay Waltons.' Well, our bishops said, 'No, we won't do that. We'll baptize you, and then you're Dunkens.' Therefore, they said, 'Well, what are we going to do?' One Dunken bishop advised them, 'Do the same thing as we did in Austria when we organized, that is, cast lots and on whom the lot falls, that person will baptize the leader and then have the leader baptize all the rest.' That is exactly what they did. That is how the River Brotherhood, the New Brotherhood in Christ was organized. But the group was now different from us."

Pfalz sipped his coffee and nodded to a young man who had sat across from us. The young man got up and beat a hasty retreat.

"We were finding more and more that outside influences were trying to change us into something we were not. For example, there was also the mode of our baptism. That was the main disagreement between us Dunkens and the influx of Papist Sprinklers. That caused a great deal of discussion and a great debate in those days. Now, of course, we Dunkens could go along with the Papists a good way because at least you understood the fact that baptism means immersion and immersion means baptism. So you were right that far. However, there was always this matter of forward or backward immersion that kept dividing us. The story I like is one my grandmother told me. She did not say who it was but it was probably one of the preachers at Little Creek during the time of this debate back and forth (whether the forward action was correct or whether the backward action was correct).

The preacher at Little Creek got up one Sunday morning and said, '*There's only one thing in all of Scripture that was ever done backwards and that's when Eli fell backwards off his chair and then he broke his neck.*' With that statement, he meant to settle the matter of the backward or the forward mode. It didn't settle anything! It served only to polarize us!" Pfalz had reached his "Preaching" crescendo; he stopped and took a few moments to calm himself.

He almost seemed to laugh at his own actions. "I'm sorry I startled you," he said. "I guess when you attempt to live in radical obedience to the Bible and to the New Testament you are open to that. You're open to being accused of spiritual pride. We pride ourselves on the fact that we are more Biblical than others are or more righteous than others, that our doctrine is purer than others are."

"I sometimes think every religion carries that burden," I added lightly.

Leon smiled. "You're right, you know. Have you ever heard the Chestnut parable?"

(That was news to me). "No, I can't say that I have."

"Well, this is one of my favorite stories of all time. Now you probably won't appreciate it so much because you're the butt of it. Tell it about somebody else. Tell it about Baptists or Methodists. It's still a wonderful story. The story was told to me by great-uncle Wendell Wotts, who was Dunken singer, song leader, at Little Creek. When he moved over here near Dayford to farm, he was a singer at the congregation. At one time, he rose, I believe, in a prayer meeting to give an object lesson. On his way, he had picked up a Chestnut that had fallen from the tree. He had a hammer, and he cracked the outer shell of the Chestnut. He said, 'Now, this outer shell of the Chestnut, this is hard, and it's not worth anything. This is the Outsiders.' Then he cracked the inner shell and he said, 'Now this inner shell of the Chestnut, this is also hard and is not worth anything. These are the Papists.' Then he cracked it open and he said, 'Inside is the good kernel, and that's our people.' When he opened it up, it was rotten inside!" Pfalz had a good chuckle at himself.

"There were other problems," he continued, "We knew a group was forming to break away and there were meetings being held in Tonkton. Some of the townspeople snuck up and looked in the window and, lo and behold, they claim people were floating around inside." He said this as if it were some damning fact.

"There was more animosity between the two churches. People were expelled from the Little Creek Church because they came to the Graterford Church to worship and participated in feet washing and communion, which according to the Little Creek council was a sin. They were read out of the church. There was no alternative; we knew we had to go our separate ways to save our way of life. For most of the group, it was painful and there was resentment in that people felt they were being expelled for their more conservative beliefs. There were those who vowed that they would oppose whatever came out of the breakup – forever." Pfalz took a sip of coffee and began his wrap up.

"We swore an oath to split ourselves into two separate but equal congregations. This would allow both groups to survive and the ways of each other not be an interference with the truth."

"A new church was built – opposite the original, but as close to the original architecture as the group could endure. Finally, the new church was finished. The original, (older) church was rededicated as *Christ Evangelical Church of Christ.*"

"That's quite a story." I said, "It explains a lot – except for the cemeteries."

"Yes. As for the cemeteries. Let me just say that they were built that way out of mutual defiance. It was a way that both groups could argue that even unto death they would be opposed to each other. The act was one of putting into opposition, a challenge; a provocation;

a summons to eternal combat over their singular ideals. As
Shakespeare said, 'He breathed defiance to my ears.'"

That last statement sent a shiver down my spine, as I could
actually picture the eternal, mutual hatred these two groups must have
had. Then, the Christian within my soul reconciled that it was
probably just the "old-timers" or the stubborn ones that felt that way.
Certainly, in today's society that same sentiment would not carry on.

"Well, Mr. Harlan, does that satisfy your curiosity?"

"It does, but I have to add that I feel sad because the two
groups couldn't reach some sort of détente." I said as I finished my
coffee.

"We did what was correct to preserve our souls," Pfalz said
darkly.

"Yes, yes you did," I rose to leave. "Thank you Mr. Pfalz, I
have to be getting back."

"I hope you understand now, the way it must be. The way
privacy is to be cherished, and the true way preserved."

"Hey, I'm a Catholic. I have my own struggles." I said as I
tried to walk away.

Pfalz took my hand in his. "Then focus on your own struggles,
not anyone else's," he said as we left.

That was charming! I thought. I really needed to put these
things out of my mind. I returned to shopping and for the rest of the
vacation I tried not to think about the two churches.

At the end of the week, we were on our way home and we were
passing the churches for the last time.

"Oh look," my wife said, "a funeral."

As we slowed for the procession, I could see the freshly dug grave, in the front row, the tombstone opposite, and facing another one on the other side of the street. I remembered my thoughts in the coffee shop: *"Certainly, in today's society that same sentiment wouldn't carry on."*

Defiance

1: intentionally contemptuous behavior or attitude
2: a hostile challenge
3: a defiant act

Familiar

"…According to Christian literature, a *Familiar* is a fallen angel or demon that inhabits the body of an animal in order to help a witch with her magical spells and to make her more powerful. Some Christians believe that the *Familiar* is sent directly from the devil and can become an incubus or succubae.

A trial in 1593 records a witch's forced confession:

"…*she had three or foure impes, some called them puckrels, one like a grey cat, another like a weasel, another like a mouse...*"

Familiars can inhabit the bodies of many animal forms. Some known *Familiars* are: cats, mice, owls, insects, frogs and toads, dogs, spiders, and so on.

The most common *Familiar* known today is the cat…"[1]

The cat seemed to slink around the Priest as he stood before the assembly.

"I want you all to know that I will do my best as your Pastor, and no one should feel that they cannot approach me for whatever reason." Father Corona said. "I am here to be of service to all your needs".

The cat let out a mournful yowl and the crowd giggled.

---

[1] *"What is a Familiar?"* by Eliza Yetter, 2003.

"Ah yes, I almost forgot to introduce you to Timothy", Father Corona reached down and lifted the cat for all to see.

"Timothy was given to me by the Bishop, with the express instructions that I keep him with me at all times. Timothy is not an 'outdoor cat', you understand. Timothy is very special to the Bishop and the Archdiocese. We will do our best to take Timothy into our hearts." The cat hissed and leapt from the priest's grasp.

"Timothy certainly knows how to make an impression doesn't he?" Father Corona said.

A few in the congregation managed an uneasy laugh.

"I hope you will all join me in the parish center for coffee and cakes, provided by the ladies sodality", Father Corona ended by pointing towards the large double doors at the side of the vestibule.

He bent down and picked up Timothy who had been cowering under a pew.

"Timothy, remember Jesus loves you, and behave yourself. I'm going to put you in your room". With that, the priest disappeared for a few moments.

...It was almost a month later when the parishioners next saw Timothy. It happened that there was an evening service on the week before Halloween. Two altar servers, Matthew Nichols and Andrew Coving were lighting the candles around the main altar when Timothy ran from the vestibule towards the main aisle of the Church. He had almost made it to the front of the aisle when Father Corona, half vested, intercepted him from a side aisle. The priest stood in front of the cat with a crucifix raised at chest level.

"Timothy! Go back to the Sacristy!" Father Corona ordered.

The cat stopped so fast he almost flipped over. He hissed and raised a paw as if to claw at the priest.

"Timothy! Let's not make a scene, go back to the Sacristy", this time Father Corona pointed the crucifix in the direction of the door to the sacristy.

"I can get him, if you want Father", Matthew said as he snuffed out the brass candle lighter.

"No, Matthew, this is between Timothy and me. We will be fine". Father Corona advanced towards the cat.

Timothy hissed once more, but moved into the sacristy.

"You can close the door when you return to the sacristy", Father Corona added.

Matthew nodded and closed the door behind himself.

As Father Corona turned to go back to the sacristy, he saw a figure in the back of the church. It appeared to be an elderly woman dressed entirely in black, with a veil over her face. She seemed to turn to look at the priest, but just as quickly, she fled through the large double doors at the end of the main aisle. A few of the other parishioners, who were scattered in the pews, turned to look at what the priest was staring at, but the woman in black had already disappeared; they only saw the doors slowly closing.

In the sacristy, Matthew watched as Timothy jumped up on the windowsill. The cat paced back and forth with its tail erect. Suddenly something outside caught its eye and the cat put both front paws on the class and began to claw as if it were trying to get out. Curious, Matthew looked out the window and saw a hunched over figure standing on the sidewalk looking back at him. The person was dressed entirely in black and their face was covered with a veil, yet, when the figure raised its head (as if to acknowledge his stare), Matthew thought he saw yellow, glowing eyes watching him.

The door on the sacristy opened and Andrew stuck his head inside.

"Is Timothy still here?" He asked.

The cat was not moving away from the window but Matthew did.

"Andy, I think there's a witch outside!" Matthew said.

"Yeah, sure", Andy moved over to the window. When he looked out, he saw nothing but the empty street below. "You're a jerk!" he said as he hit Matthew in the shoulder.

Matthew looked outside, and no one was there.

...Father Corona looked around the room one more time before he picked up the phone.

"Jack, she found out somehow. She came for Timothy, just before vespers tonight", he said half-whispering.

Timothy jumped up on the table and stared at the priest. Father Corona pushed the cat aside.

"Are you certain it's the right time for Cancelli?" Timothy began pacing across the desktop. "Yes, I know it is your call...I will expect him tomorrow morning. Good night Bishop Martin, may God be with us."

"Deus, in adiutorium meum intende. Domino, ad adiuvandum me festina".[2] Father Corona prayed as he hung up the phone.

…The doorbell ringing was followed by the housekeeper entering Father Corona's library.

Father, there is a Mister Cancelli here to see you. He said he is from Bishop Martin's Office of Special Works". She handed Father Corona a business card.

"Please send him in, Sarah."

There were footsteps in the hall and Martello Cancelli walked into the library.

"Martello, good to see you again!" Father Corona said as he came to meet the man.

"Good to see you too, you *'face brute*[3], it's a long way from Passaic, Father Mike." They shook hands warmly. "The Bishop says you have a real imbroglio on your hands."

"Yes, she wants her *Familiar* back". Father Corona said as he motioned to a chair and sat down.

"Then I say we ask her over and make a serious offer, the *Familiar* for the girl."

"I am not sure she will go for that, this is one determined person, remember she came all the way from Ireland", Father Corona

[2] "O God, come to my assistance! O Lord, make haste to help me!"
[3] Literally: 'Ugly Face'

53

could see Timothy standing in the doorway, his ears were cocked as if he were listening to their every word.

"Maybe, Maybe so, but we each have something the other wants. I think it is either going to go down our way or her way, and I know we will lose big time if it is her way." Cancelli took a glance out the window.

"Can that cat understand us"? He asked. "There is a very forlorn lady standing in the driveway right now."

"I'm not certain, but it is at the door, listening." Father Corona said.

"I say we do this, and we do it soon. We have a real problem in six days – Halloween". Cancelli watched as the woman in the driveway nodded her head. He reached across and grabbed Timothy by the scruff of his neck. The cat hissed and let out a mournful yell.

"Of course we can always take the old cat in the bag to the river trip. You would not like that would you?" He said as he shook Timothy.

Father Corona was becoming nervous at all this. He knew Martello was not a patient person, and he knew Martello had no qualms about killing the *Familiar* if he had to.

"Let us see if we can get a meeting."

Cancelli held the cat up to the window; he drew his forefinger across his throat in a menacing gesture. The woman outside seemed to be startled by his actions.

"I guaranty we will have a meeting. Now, where do you keep this critter's cage? He needs some quiet time while we talk."

Timothy was placed in the wire carrier and placed in Father Corona's bedroom.

...Two days passed without word from the mystery woman. Father Corona was once again saying vespers. He had just begun the *Magnificat*...

"My soul doth magnify the Lord. And my spirit hath rejoiced in God my Savior." There was a flash of light, like lightning, but no sound followed. Father Corona was "lifted" from himself and felt as if he were suspended above the altar. He could look down and see "himself" continuing the prayers.

"Because He hath regarded the humility of His handmaid; for behold from henceforth all generations shall call me Blessed."

"You are a very clever man, Michael Corona. You know I have little power over you in this place of torture. I have come for what is mine, the one you call Timothy. The one you see as a cat. He is mine for my pleasure. I am not an unreasonable person, unlike my master who shows no mercy to those who oppose his ways. I will be willing to trade, not in this place, but in the place I choose..." The voice was soft, yet hurtful to Father Corona's ears.

"Because He that is mighty, hath done great things to me; and holy is His name."

The voice howled in displeasure.

"And His mercy is from generation unto generations, to them that fear Him."

"I wish it were mine to decide to kill you. Oh, master this pains me so! Tomorrow at midnight, come to the Great Boulder in the

park, bring the one you call Timothy and I will have the girl with me. We will trade, and then no mercy will be shown you."

"He hath showed might in His arm: He hath scattered the proud in the conceit of their heart."

"EEEEY! It is too much for me to hear, I cannot bear it!"

"He hath put down the mighty from their seat, and hath exalted the humble".

"Bring your friend, if you must, but he should know his life is of no concern to us, except for the pleasure of the master I serve."

"He hath filled the hungry with good things; and the rich He hath sent empty away."

"You people make me sick with your wailing and please for protection. Nothing can protect you from the master. Now go, and remember, midnight tomorrow".

"He hath received Israel his servant, being mindful of his mercy".

There was another flash of light, and father Corona was "back in himself".

"…As He spoke to our fathers, to Abraham and to His seed forever…"

"Amen" responded the assembled.

…Martello and father Corona stood beside the small pond.

"Do you think you can make it here in the dark"? Cancelli asked.

"God will be with us. That I know. I will make it." Father Corona said as he took a small sack of salt from his coat pocket.

"Then we do it this way." Cancelli added.

Father Corona placed the salt on the edge of the pond and knelt down.

"Our help is in the name of the Lord. Who made heaven and earth…I EXORCIZE thee, created element of salt, by the living God, by the true God, by the holy God, by God Who by the hand of Eliseus the prophet mingled thee with water in order that the barrenness thereof might be healed; that thou may it be made salt from which the evil spirit hath been cast forth for the health of the faithful, and may it bring to all who partake of thee health of soul and body: and that there may be banished from the place in which thou shall be sprinkled, every kind of hallucination and wickedness, or craft of devilish deceit, and every unclean spirit, in the name of Him Who will come to judge the living and the dead and the world by fire."

"AMEN", Cancelli answered.

"Let us pray…We humbly entreat, O God, Thy boundless mercy and love for us, to bless and hallow this created element of salt, which Thou hast given to mankind for health of mind and body to all who partake of it, and that everything touched or sprinkled with it may be freed from all uncleanness, and from all assaults of wicked spirits. Through our Lord…" Father corona placed his hand in the water.

"I EXORCIZE thee, created element of water, in the name of God the Father almighty, and in the name of Jesus Christ His Son our Lord, and in the power of the Holy Ghost; that thou may it be made water from which the evil spirit hath been driven out for the banishment of every power of the enemy, that thou may it be able to uproot and cast out entirely that enemy himself, together with his rebel angels, by the power of the same Lord Jesus Christ, Who will come to judge the living and the dead and the world by fire."

"AMEN", Cancelli answered.

"Let us pray….O God, Who for the salvation of the human race did ordain Thy greatest Sacraments in the substance of water; graciously hearken to our prayers, and impart to this element which hath in manifold ways been purified, Thy power and blessing; so that this creature of Thine may be used in Thy mysteries and endowed with divine grace to drive away devils and to cast out diseases; that whatever in the houses or possessions of the faithful shall be sprinkled by this water, may be freed from everything unclean and hurtful. Let no spirit of pestilence or baleful breath abide therein. Let all the snares of the enemy who lieth in wait for us be driven forth, and let everything that threatens the safety or peace of the dwellers therein be banished by the sprinkling of this water: so that the health, which they seek by calling upon Thy holy name, may be guarded from all assault. Through our Lord…"

Father Corona stood, opened the sack, and put the salt three times in the water crosswise, saying:

"Let salt and water be mingled together in the name of the Father and of the Son and of the Holy Ghost.

"AMEN", Cancelli answered.

Father Corona knelt again.

"The Lord be with you. And with thy spirit. Let us pray…O God, the giver of invincible strength and king of irresistible power, ever wonderful in triumph, Who holds in check the power of the enemy, Who overcomes him fiercely going about as a roaring lion, Who by Thy might gains the victory over all his guile: we humbly pray and beseech Thee, O Lord, to look upon this Thy creation of salt and water, to bless it in Thy mercy and hallow it with the dew of Thy loving kindness: that wherever it shall be sprinkled and Thy holy name shall be invoked in prayer, every assault of the unclean spirit may be baffled, the poison of the serpent cast out, and the presence of the Holy Ghost everywhere vouchsafed to us who entreat Thy mercy. Through our Lord...in the unity of the same Holy Ghost".

"AMEN", Cancelli answered.

Father Corona stood and brushed the leaves off his clothing.

"See you tonight, Father", Cancelli said as he shook the priest's hand.

"Vaya con dios, Martello", the priest said.

...There was just enough of a wind to make the night chilly.

Father Corona held Timothy, still in the carrier, from the car to the meeting place. He new Cancelli would be nearby – he new Cancelli had an understanding of the tactics necessary.

It was easy to find the boulder, even in the darkness. It seemed to stand out like a mountain in the small clearing. Father Corona moved cautiously in the last few feet, he wanted to position himself for the run to the pond. He could barely make out the water in the distance. It was less than fifty feet away, but the expanse seemed dark and foreboding.

Midnight, and Timothy stirred hard against the edges of the carrier. The night sounds stopped abruptly.

There were footsteps and grunts from the left. Father Corona could see two shapes rapidly approaching. One was the woman in black, and the other, smaller, was a young girl being pulled along.

As they approached the boulder, Father Corona saw two yellow eyes peering from beneath the covering of the woman's face.

"So, you came alone. Trusting soul." The woman said to Father Corona.

Timothy let out a plaintive mewl.

"Yes, my friend, soon we shall be together." The woman stopped short of Father Corona. The wind had quieted and everything was icy cold and dead still. Father Corona put the cage on the ground.

"Look who they sent to get you", the woman pushed the girl in front of her, "not even your uncle himself, but some lackey".

The girl let out a shuddering cry.

"Make the exchange", Father Corona said.

"Of course. Go see your priest friend." The woman released her grip on the girl.

Father Corona opened the cage and Timothy shot out like a rocket towards the woman.

The girl hugged Father Corona.

"It is going to be fine, stay with me, Angelica, stay with me". The girl nodded assent.

Timothy had jumped up into the woman's outstretched arms and was furiously licking her face.

"Oh my pretty kitty! Come on now, we have to kill the priest and his little friend." The woman threw off her hood and raised her hands towards Father Corona.

Father Corona felt a stabbing pain in his chest. He scooped Angelica off the ground and began to run towards the pond.

"You fool! Why make it harder on the both of us? Come on, Timothy, we need some fun!"

Twenty feet to go, and Father Corona could hear the woman directly behind him. She was panting loudly and Timothy seemed to be running ahead of them both.

Ten feet to go, and Timothy stopped and turned to face the priest. There was a clap of thunder and Timothy seemed to grow before father Corona's eyes into an enormous demon. Angelica screamed.

"I would have been easy on you Father. However, the master has no pity for anyone. Especially since you held him captive. Master, my sacrifice to you, Father Michael Corona and Bishop Martin's niece, Angelica. Meet my master".

The demon pulsed with energy and Father Corona stopped short. For a moment they stared at each other. Father Corona watched as the beast's sneer slowly turned to a look of realization and horror.

A voice came out of the darkness.

"I command you, in the name of Jesus Christ, Son of the Lord, to leave this place now!" Bishop Martin stood beside the demon with his hands at his chest, palms facing outwards. There was a flash of light and a thunderclap, and the demon was gone.

"Oh my"! The woman said. "I guess I did not see that coming." She began to back away, only to be grabbed by Martello Cancelli, and pushed towards the water.

"You stink! You smell like death!" She howled. "Oh master! They are killing me! S-o-o-o-o-!" With a huge foaming splash, the two of them landed in the pond. For a few seconds the water boiled and then, all was quiet.

Martello Cancelli rose from the pond and walked to the waiting trio.

His face was darkened with something that looked like mud, but he smelled strongly of hazelnuts.

"Nutella", he said. "Best thing I have for this business". He wiped his hand across his forehead and put it in his mouth. "Good, too".

"My friends, thank you for helping to bring Angelica back to us. God has once again provided the tools we need to do his work". Bishop Martin said.

"Don't forget the Nutella", Cancelli added. The night sounds had returned.

Standard Curse Page

If you read anything on this page, you have activated the ancient curse of the "Flatulatus Impromptus" – you will expel noxious gas during any business presentation you make for seven years.

"*Where are we now, daddy?*"

For: Alexandra

FOREWORD

The *Corrigan Effect* in HyperLuminel travel considers navigational errors, their consequences, and results. It is named after the infamous American pilot, Douglas Corrigan - his alleged navigational error remains as the greatest admitted blunder of all time.

"…The story about *Wrong Way Corrigan* is the saga of Douglas Corrigan, a brash American pilot with a penchant for exaggeration and daring (stupid?) feats of flight. Forbidden by aviation authorities to fly across the Atlantic Ocean; Corrigan applied for, and received permission for a non-stop East -West crossing of America.

….It was a foggy morning. The plane was so weighed down with fuel that it traveled 3,200 feet down the runway before leaving the ground. When it passed the eastern edge of the airfield, it was only 50 feet above the ground. Not long after that, it disappeared into the fog bank, heading east. Corrigan flew into the haze and disappeared. Twenty-eight hours later, he landed in Dublin, Ireland and instantly became a national hero. Confronted by the authorities, given his unauthorized landing, Corrigan knew this was a key moment. He smiled and explained that he had taken off from Floyd Bennett Field—heading east.

'It was a very foggy morning', he pointed out to his interrogators.

He also claimed his main compass was broken—the liquid had somehow leaked out, and he had had to use a backup compass. When he finally emerged from the clouds 26 hours later, he saw only ocean.

'I looked down at the compass, and now that there was more light I noticed I had been following the wrong end of the magnetic needle on the whole flight. As the opposite of west is east, I realized that I was over the Atlantic Ocean somewhere!'

'That's my story,' said the pilot, 'but I sure am ashamed of that navigation'..." [4]

"Where are we now, daddy?"
CHAPTER_01 – THE LITTLEFIELD ARRIVES:
0, 0, 0

The memory of staring out the observation portal and seeing "nothing", a void, deep blackness not penetrated by any star or luminescence; was more than Captain Charles Waymoth was willing to accept. He was unable to recognize the obvious, somehow he and his crew were the first ever to return to earth (0, 0, 0) and not find the small blue planet in its rightful place.

In 2,782 years and untold millions of HyperLuminel jaunts, no ship had ever returned to this – absolutely nothing.

---

[4] http://www.centennialofflight.gov/essay/Explorers Record Setters and Daredevils /corrigan/EX16.htm

"Where are we now, daddy?" Jonathan asked as he tugged at his father's sleeve.

Captain Waymoth awoke from his stupor. He looked down at his son and said.

"I'm not sure, Jonathan, but I'm going to find out." Waymoth turned to the officer standing beside him.

"Bill", he said, "assemble the Guidance Team in the Ready Room. And have them look out the window before they try to BS us with some esoteric philosophy."

"Yes sir", Commander William Luckout said. He, himself took one last look at the void before he left the observation room.

"Jonathan why don't you find your mother and let her know I'll be in a meeting".

"Can I tell her about the nothing?" Jonathan asked. At his age, he was aware that something was not quite right, but he was unable to put it into the best context.

"Sure, you can tell her what you saw. Ask her if she'd like to see it herself", Captain Waymoth gave Jonathan a wink.

As soon as his son was out the door Waymoth turned, back to the void and stared for a long time…

"Where are we now, daddy?"

CHAPTER_02 – BACK TO BASICS

Guidance Member 3rd class Andrew Scatta was puzzled by what he saw. Although the celestial globe indicated a direct intersection with 0, 0, 0, there was nothing visible on the scanner screen. This was not his first HyperLuminel jaunt; it was (about) his four hundredth…it was, however, the first time he was unable to scan for earth.

There was a legend, at least that's the way it was taught in Guidance School, that a ship *had* gone out and never came back (which could be explained by 'missing' 0, 0, 0) but later incidents had shown that even if that happened (which it wouldn't) eventually the ship would show up *somewhere*. Being in a "void" just did not happen – "we all have to be somewhere", his Guidant Instructor had said.

Scatta felt both intrigued and alarmed. His mind seemed to be racing for an answer. Was this a form of spatial madness or simply human panic? He forced himself to start thinking from the beginning of his training (as he had been trained to do in an emergency); hopefully he would come across a logical explanation for all of this. He went back in his memory to Guidance 101; the course he had taken at the Sandusky Ohio Astrological Vocational Training Center.

Guidant Instructor Zavis was speaking, the room was hot, and Scatta kept falling asleep…

"…[5]Space is the three dimensional representation of everything we observe and everything that occurs. Space allows objects to have lengths in the left/right, up/down, and forward/backward directions.

Time is a fourth dimension. In normal life, time is a tool we use to measure the procession of events of space. However, time is

---

[5] *How Special Relativity Works* by John Zavisa:
http://www.howstuffworks.com/relativity.htm

something more. Yes, we use time as a 'tool', but time is essential for our physical existence. Space and time when used to describe events cannot be clearly separated. Therefore, space and time are woven together in a symbiotic manner. Having one without the other has no meaning in our physical world. To be redundant, without space, time would be useless to us and without time, space would be useless to us. This mutual dependence is known as the *Space - Time Continuum*. It means that any occurrence in our universe is an event of Space and Time. In Special Relativity, space-time does not require the notion of a universal time component. The time component for events that are viewed by people in motion with respect to each other will be different. Space-time is the death of the concept of simultaneity.

Different observers moving at different velocities (different frames of reference) will get different measurements of the same object and all of them will be correct. Special Relativity rejects the idea of any absolute ("unique" or "special") frame of reference; rather physics must look the same to **all** observers traveling at a constant velocity (inertial frame).

Here is an important fact about reference frames: There is no such thing as an absolute frame of reference in our universe. By saying absolute, what is actually meant is that there is no place in the universe that is stationary. This statement says that since everything is moving, all motion is relative. Think about it - the earth itself is moving, so even though you are standing still, you are in motion. You are moving through both space and time at all times. Because there is no place or object in the universe that is stationary, there is no single place or object on which to base all other motion..."

"Guidance Member Scatta, report to the Ready Room". The intercom syntho-vox disturbed Andrew's concentration. This event was real, he thought. (Time to solve the puzzle)! The trip to the Ready Room would take several minutes. Andrew strapped himself into a transport chair and returned to the lecture…

"Where are we now, daddy?"

CHAPTER_03 – THE CONSTANTS "AREN'T"

Guidant Scatta entered the Ready Room and saw that the assembled staff had "worried" expressions on their faces. The trip had been uneventful until now. There was the unexplained "bump" last night, but everything else seemed to be normal.

"Guidant Scatta", Captain Waymoth said, "Where are we?"

"Captain we are at 0, 0, 0. That much I know, but as to earth not being visible to us, it could be anything from a light block to a halo."

"Guidant Scatta, can you explain to the Social Officers what the procedure is to resolve this so they can best communicate it to the ship's company?"

"Yes Captain I will. There are nine premises that are used to derive the navigational constants we use for travel…

The first premise is that the *initial point of departure is not fixed.* It is always relative to the starting point 0, 0, 0 – and it is redefined as needed based on other variable parameters[6].

---

[6] 0, 0, 0 is always an inertial location – based on time.

The second premise is referred to as the *'cumulative effects'* premise and considers the variables over time such as:

Gravity waves

Orbital Decay

Large "Mass" influences

Space resistance

Unknown Perturbations

The third premise is the *'Columbus Cube[7]'* which is the spatial area where 0, 0, 0 <u>should</u> be at the return, considering the *'cumulative effects'*.

The fourth premise is the *'Corrigan effect[8]'* – it considers navigational errors and their results.

The fifth premise is the *'Code 5' premise* –you are in the right place at the right time, but 0, 0, 0 somehow does not exist.

The sixth premise addresses the fact that: *Unexpected occurrences happen!* These occurrences can take the form of cosmic catastrophes, never receiving news, or never receiving software locational updates.

The seventh premise states that *you do not know if you are too early or too late in arrival.* If you are too early, the object may still be approaching your location – in that case how long do you wait for a correction? If you are too late, the object has passed your rendezvous point and you will never 'see it'.

The eighth premise discusses what is *'close'* or *'nearby'*? Is it one astronomical unit? Is it a greater or lesser number? Is it sensor range?"

---

[7] Columbus "Knew" the earth was round; he never realized how round (big) it was.
[8] Named for Douglas "wrong way" Corrigan.

The ninth, or final premise is that our reality is no longer synchronized with our origin and we are, in fact, at the 0, 0, 0, but not in the same 'sense'.

Remember the basic elements of motion are extremely complex, even for the planet earth. The earth orbits around the sun at a rate of (approximately) 18.51 miles per second, in a tilted elliptical plane, while the sun travels around the galaxy at (approximately) 140 miles per second, in its own path, while the galaxy itself moves through space at (approximately) 190 miles per second, in its own path. There is a (combined) 350 mile per second error rate, making the *initial* Columbus Cube 42,875,000 cubic miles!

Therefore, we present a theory of movement of objects in space: as the so-called 'Grand View'.

❖ Earth goes around the sun @ 18.5 miles per second.

❖ Solar system is moving towards constellation Hercules @ 12 miles per second.

❖ Forward speed of Solar System around the Milky Way is 144 miles per second.

❖ Milky Way (itself) is moving toward Andromeda Galaxy @ 80 miles per second.

❖ Local galaxies are all headed for "The Great Attractor" (a mysterious concentration of mass beyond the constellation Virgo).

None of this is 'straight-line' travel; it is more like a rifle bullet, slowly twisting as is moves. In addition, there are 'gravitational eddies' that exacerbate the twists and turns". Scatta was relieved that he had gotten all the information out in such a simplistic form.

"There is a margin of error for all this", Captain Waymoth added. "Guidant Scatta and his staff will be analyzing the data and will have an answer shortly. At this time, there should be no cause for undue alarm. Questions?"

Duration courtesy made most of the Social Officers quiet. Social Officer Intercessor stood up.

"I know it's not our place, Captain Waymoth, but if we could have some understanding of HyperLuminel Travel it would help us formulate a set of FAQs".

"Social Officer Intercessor, you realize there is no easy explanation. I can, however, call-up this tutorial..." Captain Waymoth pointed at the "white wall".

An image appeared followed by a voice over...

"I am Dr. Placker, and I'll do my best to give you a simplified overview of HyperLuminel Travel. Keep in mind that what I say is only the simplistic approach...

From orbit (which we have reached by ascending from the ground on pseudo gravity repulsors), your starship accelerates on thrusters toward the point where it will enter hyperspace, and decelerates to rest there. This onramp is along the axis of rotation of the local star, about 0.5 to 1 light hour out (depending on the size of the star and the quality of the ship), so the trip will take a few days.

Once in hyperspace, the trip to the edge of the system takes several hours, possibly as much as a day for very slow ships, and the inward trip at the destination system takes an equal amount of time, but the journey between systems rarely occupies more than an hour. At the destination system, the ship emerges from hyperspace and travels to the destination planet, either orbiting or landing once it arrives. The total time elapsed is on average about five days, but varies widely depending not only on the length of the route but also the quality of the ship and pilot.

Like aircraft, near-orbit spacecraft use pseudo gravity repulsors for propulsion. A repulsor is nothing more than a pseudo gravity generator that produces a very large, very diffuse field, which by reacting weakly against the immense mass of a planet produces useful amounts of force on the generator without harmful or even noticeable effects on the surroundings. Although a repulsor field is very large, it is not infinitely so: thrust declines with altitude in a complicated but monotonic way and drops to effectively zero at about one planetary radius. This is well outside any reasonable safety limit for thrusters, however.

A lengthy but necessary digression on the structure of Hyperspace is somewhat complicated. To begin with, it comes in two flavors, bound and free. Bound, or fixed, hyperspace is that associated with a star. The region of bound hyperspace around a star is roughly spherical, with a radius of approximately 4 light hours times the square root of the star's mass (in solar masses); outside that limit is free hyperspace. Free hyperspace is not just the bound hyperspace of the galaxy as a whole; it is qualitatively different. In particular, it is "fluid" enough for ships to enter it fully ("to accept hyper mass converted from Einsteinian mass-energy" in physicist-speak).

Where bound and free hyperspace meet is a turbulent region called the "hyper pause", which surrounds the star. Over the rotational poles of the star, the "hyper pause" extends inward to the star, in two cones of lesser turbulence called the onramps. The onramps are an intermediate form of hyperspace, which ships can enter, but where they cannot travel faster than light (and in practice must travel slower due to the turbulence. The width of an onramp at any point is between $1/8^{th}$ and ¼ the distance from the center of the star, depending on how fast the star spins.

Fast travel within a solar system is provided by "reaction less" thrusters, which actually react against the mass of the local star through bound hyperspace. (Thrusters also operate in free hyperspace; it is unclear what they are reacting against in that case.) The force provided is very large: modern spacecraft, with their crews protected by compensatory pseudo gravity fields, accelerate at tens or hundreds of gravities.

The limitation of the thruster is that it cannot couple to the local hyperspace if their relative velocity differs by too much. The intrinsic velocity of bound hyperspace is very close to that of the star; free hyperspace has something like the average of nearby stars. The critical velocity depends on how well the thruster is tuned, which in turn depends on its basic quality, how well maintained it is, and how large it is.

Smaller thrusters are easier to keep in good tune, so permit higher final velocities, but provide less thrust and therefore lower acceleration for a given payload. Since multiple thrusters automatically have pathetic tuning, smaller ships are in general faster than large ones (given an equivalent drive: payload ratio). A typical critical velocity, for a small freight or passenger ship with average maintenance, is about 4000 km/s (0.8 light-minutes per hour). Large freighters or dreadnaughts might go as low as 1500 km/s, while small one- or two-person scouts or couriers might reach 6000 km/s. Vessels with lots of manpower dedicated to continuous maintenance (such as military ships) can improve these figures by about 50%. Accelerations for civilian ships are usually on the order of 10-20 gravities (350-700 km/s per hour); military ships reach 50-150g (1800-5400 km/s per hour).

Although thrusters, like repulsors, require nothing but energy (easily provided by a fusor) to operate, they do produce dangerous amounts of high-frequency electromagnetic radiation and conspicuous numbers of neutrinos. This waste is emitted preferentially opposite to the direction of thrust, thus the actinic exhaust ports visible at the stern of most spacecraft. The x-rays produced pose a distinct hazard to anyone behind the ship, so most ports restrict the operation of thrusters near planets and inhabited or important facilities. Military ships often have extra equipment to redirect the emissions to where they hope enemy sensors are not, but there is always some neutrino leakage.

Entering hyperspace is easier further out on the onramp, as measured as a fraction of the distance to the hyper pause. Modern ships can make the transition at somewhere between 1/8 and ¼, the hyper pause radius, depending solely on the quality of their hyper drive: ship size is irrelevant. For a Sol-sized star, that is 30 to 60 light minutes, which takes 40-75 hours to cover at a nominal 4000 km/s (plus acceleration and deceleration).

Traveling along the onramp is always bumpy, but is much worse and actively dangerous if the ship entered hyperspace with anything other than zero relative velocity; deceleration is not optional. A ship leaving hyperspace gets whatever velocity relative to local hyperspace it had with respect to hyperspace where it entered, which by the above is usually very close to zero. Regardless of the ship's normal-space velocity, travel along the onramp is limited absolutely by the speed of light and practically by the pilot's ability to use her sensors to detect impending turbulence. As a rule of thumb, a ship with good sensors and two competent pilots can safely make 0.5c, taking 6-7 hours to reach free hyperspace. Flying the onramp takes a great deal of concentration, so standard procedure is to have two pilots switch off. A ship with not-so-good sensors, or only one pilot, should stick to 1/3 or even ¼ c, while a top-of-the line ship can reach 0.75c or even more with a sufficiently crazed pilot.

Once in free hyperspace, travel is very quick: modern ships can move at half a light-year to two or three light years' per minute. Inhabited systems would be only a few minutes apart on straight-line courses. Sadly, such courses are rarely feasible.

Free hyperspace is decidedly non-homogenous. Large sections of it are filled with the same sort of turbulence that characterizes a system's hyper pause, and this turbulence is not even necessarily fixed in position. However, it does tend to stay within certain areas, or more importantly, out of certain areas, permitting safe passage along mapped routes.

Unfortunately, modern technology does not permit safe or efficient mapping of hyperspace: the range of hyper field sensors is not enough to detect rough hyperspace from farther away than it can expand to engulf a ship. With few exceptions, hyperspace maps are left over from pre-Imperial times, and generally consist only of known safe routes, rather than complete surveys of flat and rough areas. Even this fragmentary knowledge is not evenly distributed: although public knowledge includes routes between any two systems, there are many shortcuts and alternate routes known only to a few. The prominent exception to this is the core of the Empire, a region approximately 80-

100 light-years' across which is, with the exception of a few well-known and well-mapped obstacles such as Murcher's Wall and The Muyin Pit, is completely flat. Within the Middle Provinces, interstellar travel can usually take the fastest and cheapest route, a fact not completely unrelated to the region's prosperity.

A hyper drive requires a closed shell with certain properties, and affects everything inside that shell and nothing outside it; even objects in direct physical contact with the outside of the shell are not taken into hyperspace. In modern ships, the necessary shell is provided by the hull field, so a hull field failure will prevent hyperspace travel.

If the shell becomes unenclosed while in hyperspace, the ship is never seen again. Anything that leaves the shell with the hyper drive (even though that requires a shell of its own to avoid falling under the previous sentence) is likewise gone for good. Physicists have come to blows over exactly what happens, but that it is not anything survivable is unquestioned. Ships in hyperspace can detect each other, at a range of up to several light-minutes, and can communicate at low bandwidth by varying the characteristics of their hyper drive fields. Since nothing can leave a hyper drive field and continue to exist, hyperspace combat is effectively impossible. However, contact between two hyper drive fields causes them both to fail. Safety mechanisms will usually cause the ships to fall back into normal space (probably with damaged hyper drives), but a malfunction can cause one or both to vanish forever. Some warships carry missiles with individual hyper drives to disable other ships, but this is very expensive.

The peculiar nature of hyperspace signaling means that it is ineffectual beyond a few light minutes; interstellar radio is not possible by any techniques currently known, or even known to the Republic.

Dedicated couriers that travel from onramp to onramp, delivering and receiving messages by laser to avoid having to travel to the local planet, can cut out most or all of the overhead time, but the speed of hyperspace travel is still the upper limit on the speed of information between systems…"

The screen became white again.

"I don't know if that was any help to you, but it is the least complex explanation we can provide", Captain Waymoth added.

An Intercessor rose from his seat. He wore his emoticon mask, but he was clearly spirited.

"So we are lost, and there is no easy way to determine how, or what happened. Is there hope, Captain? Can I tell my populace there is hope?"

Another Intercessor stood and raised his hand in front of his chest, palm forward.

"Clearly, Koalemos, if we are discussing this, there is hope. We are still sentient. At least I feel a challenge".

"Get a life, Hecate", Koalemos said.

"Please, if you need time to discuss this, we must return to our duties", Captain Waymoth motioned toward Scatta.

"Of course, Captain, a quick solution will benefit all", Hecate said.

Captain Waymoth and Guidant Scatta left the room. Scatta turned to go down the walk tube, but Waymoth grabbed his arm.

"Fix this – that's an order!" Captain Waymoth said.

"Captain, I intend to, it's my ass too", Guidant Scatta answered.

"Where are we now, daddy?"

CHAPTER_04 – THE "9ᵗʰ PREMISE"

Guidant Scatta sat back in his chair. He had reviewed all the data, the logs, and run 125 different simulations…the answer was "not good".

"Captain Waymoth, I need to see you in steerage. Guidant Scatta". (This was one conversation he did not want to have).

He could not help but remember the eloquent summation that was written on the wall of the main lecture hall of the Sandusky Ohio Astrological Vocational Training Center:

"…***Here are the concepts you have discovered during your six years of training:***

1. ***There is no such thing as an absolute (stationary) frame of reference.***

2. ***The laws of physics apply equally to all frames of reference.***

3. ***The speed of light is constant in all frames of reference.***

4. ***There is no simultaneity of events between separate frames of reference.***

Guidants: Do not fall prey to these errant statements:

1. ***Time slows as speed increases. (Only when viewed by another frame of reference)***

2. ***Objects shorten as speed increases. (Same as above)***

3. ***Special Relativity cannot handle acceleration. (Biggest***

misconception about Special Relativity)

4. Mass increases with speed. (Energy increases, not the rest mass)

5. Nothing can travel faster than the speed of light.

6. Crossing the speed of light barrier from either a faster or a slower speed is disallowed...''

Somehow, the Littlefield had managed to violate the 9th premise.

The door swung open and Captain Waymoth walked in.

"I don't imagine it is goods news since you contacted me on the personal band". He said.

"We are alive. We are at 0, 0, 0. We are not in the same plane of reference, we have been 'shifted out of phase'...

"Let me hear all of it, then", Waymoth, said as he sat in the visitor's chair.

"Because of our drive design, any phase-shift is reduced to zero since the magnetic moments are kept parallel with each other.

We know that a phase-shift could originate from a weak miss-tracking effect when conduction electron 'spins' lag behind the magnetic moments in the domain-wall - in our case, the hyper drive shell.

The most commonly described case is when the wave function of a charged particle passing around a long solenoid experiences a 'phase shift' because of the enclosed magnetic field, despite the magnetic field being zero in the region through which the particle passes.

This formulation allows a more natural description of the Aharonov-Bohm effect in which a charged particle is affected by regions with different electrical potentials but zero electric field. In this system a magnetic field shielded by a long super conducting tube defines a flat (F = 0) but non-trivial connection outside of the tube.

The connection has a non-trivial holonomy along a curve encircling the tube, which corresponds to a phase shift for electrons waves traveling either side of the tube. This is detected by a double split electron diffraction experiment by changing the magnetic field. The magnetic field remains constant zero outside of the tube so is undetectable classically.[9]

At 0.62 LNU,[10] we encountered a gravitational eddy at 45^0 and 'bounced', causing us to momentarily loose reference.

The magnetization rotation direction created a phase-shift along a typical phase coherent electron trajectory of about five π .[11]

A separate 'molecular' Aharonov-Bohm effect for nuclear motion in multiply connected regions occurred, dependent only on local quantities along the nuclear path." [12]

Captain Waymoth leaned forward.

"They cannot detect us or help us in any way. The closest analogy I can come to is the historical reference to a twentieth century experiment: *The Philadelphia Experiment: A Personal Saga in Time Travel*[13].

We are where we should be, but not in the same phase reference plane so that we can be seen or detected. I cannot say if we are out of phase by a positive or negative value; although it is a moot point."

---

[9] http://en.wikipedia.org/wiki/Aharonov-Bohm effect
[10] 0.62NU = 0.62 "Luminal Night Units" OR 01:49.25 AM American Old Hours > See Discussion at end of Chapter
[11] (143.2375 degrees - could be + or - out of phase)
[12] http://en.wikipedia.org/wiki/Maxwell's equations
[13] www.spiritual-endeavors.org

"Can we correct for this? Can we return?" Captain Waymoth asked.

"It is doubtful, there is no protocol, and there is no way to recompense what we have encountered. We are where we are."

The black void that filled the viewport was unforgiving in its exhaustion.

———————————

A Note concerning USP – "Universal Space Time"

In the year 2105 (Earth), it was decided that a new measurement of time was needed to suit the needs of the impending HyperLuminel age. As a result, the (previous) 365.25-day transit of Earth around the Sun was changed to 1000 LU (Luminal Units). The 1000 LU corresponded to 8,766 OH (Old Hours). Each "Day" was 8.766 LU: simply called a "Unit". Old Midnight was "0", and Old Noon was 4.383 LU.

Deth 2 Squrrellz

Three gray squirrels raced across the dried leaves and seemed to squirm into a ball before they spiraled up the oak tree. The afternoon bus had just opened its doors and the sounds of the students had caused the disruption. Jeremy Ledger tossed an acorn into the tree and he heard the squirrels swirling around the dried branches.

"Can't get them", his brother David said. "I hate squirrels. Too much confusion".

"Well, you better watch out, they are collecting nuts at this time of year". Jeremy tossed another acorn into the canopy.

"Funny - real funny. Hey, wait, what's going on over at Mr. Wayons house?"

Jeremy turned to see a police cruiser parked in front of his neighbor's house.

"Don't know, let's go find out", together they crossed the street and walked to the hedgerow bordering the property. They could see a police officer speaking to Carl Wayons who was standing in the doorway.

From that distance, they could barely make out the conversation.

"Mr. Wayon, the chicken has to stay confined to your yard. Your neighbors don't want it roaming loose," the officer said.

Carl Wayons stood just inside the door; he was holding a red hen under one arm.

"I'm telling you it wasn't loose! That Carter woman is a busybody and she just wants to stir up some trouble", he said as he stroked the chicken with his free hand.

"Maybe, but she said she was going to file a complaint about your so-called 'artworks'", the officer swept his hand towards the yard.

"It isn't artwork; it's religion I tell you. I have a right to express my religion", Carl seemed frustrated by the accusation.

"Whatever. With all the things I have to worry about in town I don't need a neighbor fight sucking up my time", the officer paused and said, "Talk to her, maybe you two can work it out".

"I'll try, but it takes two to reach an agreement".

They shook hands and the officer left.

"Religion?" David asked after a time.

They had started walking back home. A wind caused a blizzard of brown leaves to rattle across the road and die in a pile.

"You know, that stuff mom and dad do. Church stuff". Jeremy answered.

"Oh, that. What did he mean about the artwork?"

"You have a lot of questions for a kid who can't even catch a squirrel".

A ball of grey fur exploded in front of them and chattering, it ran up the nearest tree. The squirrel paused, and began to loudly send out a warning bark.

David picked up a rock and tossed it in the direction of the sound. There was a splash in the dry leaves as the rock fell, unused. The squirrel continued to remonstrate them even as they passed by.

"I can make a list", David said as they reached the back door of their house. "I can make a list of all the artworks Mr. Wayon has around his yard".

"Then what?" Jeremy opened the mailbox and sorted through the mail.

"I'll give the list to someone who knows something. They can tell us what the things mean".

"See if they can tell you why you can't hit a squirrel with a rock", Jeremy threw the mail on the kitchen table.

"Shut up! I can and I will, just not today"…

During the next few days, David spent time each afternoon carefully making his list of the 'artwork" in Mr. Wayon's yard. David turned it into a sort of spy game. He pretended he was gathering information on the enemy to defeat the evil empire…

Just before Halloween, he happened to be adding to the list. He hid behind the stockade fence panel and peered through a broken slat. David had rewritten the list several times until it began to make sense:

2 Buckets

3 Glass Lawn Ornaments

4 Windows on one wall

5 Bricks in the side walk to the door

6 Seed canisters

7 Candles

8 Pillars

9 Pear trees

10 Chain Links

11 Pine Trees

12 Rocks

13 Steps from the cellar

14 Fence Posts in a Row

He had watched Carl Wayons fuss over each of these items. Carl touched them and seemed to pause at each one. Most of the time David saw him walk from one to the other, pausing long enough at each one to (what?) Pray? It seemed Carl always had the chicken under his arm. David though it was to prevent the bird from escaping, but them it occurred to him that each time Carl Wayon started the journey through the yard he picked up the hen, first. After watching this, he wrote the final item on his list:

1 Hen.

None of it made any sense, but he had his list. He was sure it was correct.

On that same day, he heard Mrs. Carter yelling at Mr. Wayon.

"You clean up this junk in your yard! It's ruining my property values you crazy old fool!"

Mr. Wayon stood silently; he offered no rebuttal.

"I'm going to have my son come over one night and clean it for you."

"Please leave my things alone. Please let me live in peace". Mr. Wayons said.

"You just wait until dark – I'll make sure you have a yard that's acceptable for this neighborhood."

Dave sat with his back against the fence wondering if the threats were real. He decided to tell someone, not his parents, they would yell at him for "spying". The only other person he could trust was his uncle, Larry.

Larry Defoe Ledger was Dave and Jeremy's only living relative. Dave always wondered why his mother would whisper to his father; "You know he isn't 'right'. I don't want him around the boys". Their father would simply shrug his shoulders and repeat the same phrase, "Larry has problems, but he would never bother the boys with them". Of course none of that made any sense, all Dave knew was that his uncle had been in the military and was sent home after something happened and was given a medal, "…In the name of the Congress of the United States". At least that was what the plaque said.

Dave had tried to read the plaque several times, but each time his mother told him not to "stare at that thing". Finally, he had Jeremy tell him what the paper said.

He did remember most of what it said,

"...While a member of the armed forces, Sergeant Larry Defoe Ledger, USMC, distinguished himself conspicuously by gallantry and intrepidity at the risk of his life above and beyond the call of duty while engaged in an action against an enemy of the United States; while serving with friendly foreign forces engaged in an armed conflict against an opposing armed force.

On April 18, 200 – Sergeant Defoe was in charge of a rifle platoon. Sergeant Defoe's platoon was conducting search/combat operations when the lead men in the platoon received intense small arms, automatic weapons, rocket, and mortar fire from a well-entrenched enemy force. As the platoon fought its way forward, the extremely heavy enemy fire caused numerous friendly casualties. Sensing the need for early treatment of the wounded, Sergeant Defoe quickly moved from his relatively safe position in the rear of the foremost point of the advance and made numerous trips through the enemy killing zone to move the injured men out of the danger area. Noting that a large part of the enemy fire was coming from a partially camouflaged bunker, he seized a machinegun and assaulted the key enemy location, delivering devastating fire as he advanced. He forced his way directly into the enemy strong point. Although he was seriously wounded, his fearless attack killed 18 of the enemy and drove the remainder from the bunker. Sergeant Defoe's bold actions completely disorganized the enemy defense and saved the lives of many of his comrades. His daring initiative, selfless devotion to duty, and indomitable fighting spirit, reflected great credit upon himself and the Marine Corps, and his performance upheld the highest traditions of the U.S. Naval Service. This deed exemplifies personal bravery and self-sacrifice, an action that conspicuously distinguishes this individual above his comrades. Award of this decoration is considered on the standard of extraordinary merit..."

Uncle Larry was "a hero", was all Dave could really understand. Uncle Larry would know what to do...

"Well Dave, that is quite a list," Uncle Larry said. "And you made it all without being seen".

"I hid behind the fence and watched", Dave said. "There's going to be trouble tonight, at Mr. Wayons' house. I heard Mrs. Carter say she was going to do something to make his yard acceptable".

"Well, I'm sure she was just upset about the way he keeps his property".

"Mr. Wayons told the Police officer that it wasn't 'junk', it was religion stuff".

Larry Defoe looked at the list again. He began to understand what was going on.

"I'll tell you what Dave; I'll keep an eye on things tonight. You go home and don't worry about it".

"Thanks, Uncle Larry. Will you tell us what happens?" David started out the door.

"Nothing is going to happen. Enjoy the squirrels", Uncle Larry added as he watched Dave leave. Two grey squirrels skittered across the lawn, chased by a red squirrel close at their tails. Dave tossed a stick at the trio, but they were long gone when it hit the ground...

Larry sat quietly on the front porch. Even though it was late, he did not mind either the darkness or the chill. The neighborhood seemed quiet enough. The squirrels were long gone. He had watched a solitary cat slink along the sidewalk, pause, and move into the shadows.

A light came on at the Wayons' front porch. Larry leaned over the railing to see better. There was someone in the walking around in the front yard, swinging something that looked like a baseball bat.

"*Thunk!*" The bat hit something. There was a muffled sound as another object was struck.

"Hey! What are you doing?" It was Mr. Wayons' voice. Larry saw the front door open and Wayons appeared on the porch, holding his hen under one arm. "Stop!"

Larry thought about calling the police, but he saw the person holding the bat move towards the porch. Larry vaulted over the railing and began to trot to the Wayons' house.

"You're a crazy bastard!" The assailant yelled.

Larry was in the yard, but not before he saw the intruder swing at Carl Wayons. At the same time the hen wriggled free and tried to fly away, Carl Wayons lunged to grab the animal, but he put himself directly into the path of the swinging baseball bat.

"Crack!" The bat hit Carl Wayons on the side of the head. For a second Wayons stood straight up and then went down on his face, dead.

Larry was in the yard and he could see Mrs. Carter inside the Wayons' house with a lit road flare, lighting whatever she could, on fire. She must have come in the back door when Carl went out the front. She had not yet realized her son had killed Carl Wayons.

The plan had been to create a distraction in the front yard, and when Wayons came to investigate, she would torch the house.

Her son was standing over the body, when Larry came from behind.

"Drop the bat", Larry said.

Mrs. Carter's son, Gerald, turned around, swinging the bat as he did. Larry deflected the blow with his arm, but he was still knocked off balance. He staggered back.

Mrs. Carter came out the front door, silhouetted by the growing fire. She saw Carl Wayons lying in a pool of blood, the hen pecking the ground beside him, and her son swinging wildly at Larry Defoe Ledger.

"Jesus Christ! Gerald! What are you doing? What are you doing?" She yelled.

Gerald turned halfway to face her. "I had to mom! I had to finish this!"

Larry took advantage of the moment of inattention and grabbed Gerald's legs.

The neighbors had all come running to the scene, and in the distance the wail of sirens could be heard.

At that instant everything changed for the worse.

Mrs. Carter pulled a chrome-plated pistol from her jacket pocket and approached the two men who were fighting on the ground. She pointed the pistol at them.

"Turn him over, Gerald! Turn him over!"

In a split second the tragedy became intolerable. Dave Ledger ran from the crowd and came between Mrs. Carter and the two combatants – at the same instant that Mrs. Carter fired two shots (hoping to kill Larry). Dave Ledger joined Carl Wayons in death.

Larry forced himself free, and started for Mrs. Carter. She fired at him, but her aim was off and the bullet grazed his chest. Gerald stood and grabbed Larry from behind, turning Larry enough that Mrs. Carter's next two shots hit Gerald squarely in the chest. He staggered backwards towards the crowd of onlookers, who by now, were screaming and yelling in disbelief.

At last Larry was able to lunge at Mrs. Carter and he took one more round in the shoulder before he tackled her to the ground. She lay beneath him screaming that he was a "Murderer!"

The confusion heightened as the Police and Fire Services arrived on the scene. All the neighbors were talking at the same time and the Wayons house was completely engulfed in flames.

...Jeremy watched his mother open a letter and then crumple it into a ball. She tossed it into the wastebasket and stared out the window. Tears streamed down her face and dripped onto her sweater. She stood for a long time and then seemed to "give up". She went into the living room and turned on the television. Jeremy waited until he could hear the voices; *"Now Karen you told me that when you found your husband in bed with your sister you got undressed and joined them...Well, Dr. Phil I saw they were having such..."*

It was bad for everyone with Dave gone. What made it worse was that at the inquest, Jeremy's mother insisted that Uncle Larry be "locked up" for psychiatric observation. Dad was furious with mom. After that, they did not seem like a family anymore. The judge had ordered Uncle Larry to be "taken away", and he never even said a word about anything. Two court officers took him away in shackles, but before they did, one of them handed the blue-ribboned medal to Jeremy's father.

"You are no fu----- hero now!" his mother had yelled as they took him out of the room.

Jeremy's father spent a lot of time in his brother's apartment, sometimes he even slept there. Jeremy was not sure why, but he knew his father was just as hurt as his mother was. As a matter of fact there was a lot of "talk" around town, it seemed everyone was whispering something whenever Jeremy walked by.

The burned out hulk of Mr. Wayons house still stood across the street. Jeremy had seen a young woman wandering around the yard, crying, he figured it must be Mr. Wayons daughter or something. Mrs. Carter was in prison for "twenty five to life" – that is what it said in the newspaper. Nevertheless, Uncle Larry was locked away, being "observed".

Jeremy went into the kitchen and stared at the wastebasket. The letter was from his uncle, and it was addressed to him. Jeremy listened to make certain his mother was still watching television. He could hear her sobbing, even over the audience laughter.

Finally, Jeremy took the crumpled letter out of the basket and sat down to read it:

"Dear Jeremy,

You know I am going on a long trip, one that I really cannot take you on. I will not need my truck for this one. Before I go, I want to give you the secrets to Carl Wayons 'code.'

I know that you and Dave thought he was a bit crazy, but he was just different. Carl saw things in a way we could not. Or at least in a way I could not until the night of the fire when I began thinking very hard about what was going on in my life and what would become of me.

As near as I can figure out this whole story was about what Carl believed in and what he needed to help him remember. It is tough for us older folks to mention such things to the younger ones because you just do not understand what 2,000 years of testing has to do with it.

I am going to tell you what I know and what I think. What I want you to do is think about it yourself someday, and see if we were not right:

1 Hen = The One true God revealed in the person of Jesus Christ. The single hen is Christ Jesus, the Son of God. Christ is symbolically presented as a mother hen in memory of the expression of Christ's sadness over the fate of Jerusalem: *"Jerusalem! Jerusalem! How often would I have sheltered thee under my wings, as a hen does her chicks, but thou wouldst not have it so ..."*

2 Buckets = The Old and New Testaments. Buckets, like books, hold many vital things in our lives.

3 <u>Glass Lawn Ornaments</u> = Faith, Hope and Charity. Beauty, ever changing and mysterious. Simple things that affect us all.

4 <u>Windows on one wall</u> = Four Gospels and/or the Four Evangelists. The gospels let us look into the world of Jesus and allow us to see the outside world, as we should.

5 <u>Bricks in the side walk to the door</u> = The first Five Books of the Old Testament, the "Pentateuch" which contain the law Condemning us of our sins. Worn and traveled, but reminders of the past.

6 <u>Seed canisters</u> = The 6 days of creation - Each day a new creation.

7 <u>Candles</u> = The seven gifts of the Holy Spirit & The seven sacraments of the Catholic faith

8 <u>Pillars</u> = The eight beatitudes

9 <u>Pear trees</u> = The nine "Fruits of the of the Spirit

10 <u>Chain Links</u> = The Ten Commandments

11 <u>Pine Trees</u> = The eleven faithful apostles. Tall and true, evergreen and fast against the storm.

12 <u>Rocks</u> = The twelve points of doctrine the Apostle's Creed. Never changing, substantial.

13 <u>Steps from the cellar</u> = The number of people present at the Last Supper. Each step a memory of the beginning of the great story.

14 <u>Fence Posts in a Row</u> = Stations of the Cross. Wood, they crucified him on a wooden cross.

> Keep the faith,
>
> Uncle Larry

...Two grey squirrels crossed the yard; it was a beautiful spring day, time to play in the sunshine.

www

Chapter – 1 – You have reached bandwidth[14]

"...We are the Borg. Lower your shields, and surrender your ship. We will add your biological and technological distinctiveness to our own. Your culture will adapt to service ours. Resistance is futile..."
Star Trek

They were kneeling in front of his car. Two "spacemen" in some kind of suits were kneeling in supplication. Their arms were held apart as if they were asking for divine intervention. T.C. Web was fortunate he was driving the Audi and not his delivery truck. He laid on the brake pedal and the car stopped dead, not more than two feet in front of the two "men".

He assumed they were men, although at this distance they could have been women. He wasn't sure of anything at this point. All he knew was that there was a bright flash and these two were kneeling in the middle of the road.

"...Lenny, I'll call you right back. I got a situation here," T.C. said into his mouthpiece. He focused the

---

[14] Bandwidth denotes the amount of information exchanged between units and to which mental depth it occurs. The extreme case is total connection where the bandwidth is so high that all units form a single neural network.

dashboard camera on them and began recording as soon as he stepped out of the vehicle.

"You fellas OK?" he asked from just behind the driver's side door. They looked at him and seemed to blink their eyes.

"It is true. I am Three of Nine. You are Gods!" One of them said as they stood.

"I am Eight of Ten", the other one said. "You have reached bandwidth. You are Gods!"

"I'm T.C. Web. The T.C. means Terrance Commodious – I like just T.C. myself." He was speed-dialing 911.

"9-1-1 You are being recorded...What is your emergency?"

"This is T.C. Web on route 402 East near Wydot Road, are you receiving my dash-cam image?"

"Sir, is this a joke?"

"It's not joke, I almost ran over these two guys in the middle of the road."

"And they are?"

"I am Three of Nine".

"I am Eight of Ten".

"Sir, I have your position and your vehicle ID. I want you all to remain where you are until the officers arrive".

"We Borg, seek contact with the Gods", Three of Nine said.

"You have reached bandwidth. You are Gods!" Eight of Nine added.

"Yeah, OK. I'll be here, but hurry up, this is really creeping me out". T.C. stepped around the door and made a movement towards the two figures.

He brought out his cell phone and hit the web button. Nimbly he sent a text message to CNN, "Live Feed" and turned on the cell camera. "I hope you're getting this", he said under his breath (it was worth a least $5,000 if it made the hourly broadcast, more if it was a feature story).

"Hello, ah...Three of Nine". T.C. extended his hand.

"I am Eight of Ten."

"OK, sorry about that; Eight of ten".

"You will allow us to touch you?" Eight of ten asked.

"Sure, you can. You don't have any strange diseases, do you?"

"What is a disease?" Three of Nine said.

"You know, a virus, a bug."

Both Borg recoiled in horror and fell to their knees.

"You must think us to be inferior. The Borg was once the victim of a virus, but we have purged it from the collective."

A state police cruiser was rapidly approaching from behind T.C.'s car. The blue lights and strobes were reflected in the chest shields of the spacesuits.

"This device is attractive to the collective". Three of Nine said.

A trooper approached, while his partner assumed a defensive position near the car.

"What is this unit?" Eight of ten asked.

"He's a Police Officer." T.C. explained. "He investigates. He keeps the order."

The Borg conferred. T.C. heard them say "He is like the 'Borg Queen', He brings order into chaos". They stood at attention.

"OK, wise guys, what's going on here?" the trooper said.

"The Borg does not understand police officer." Three of Nine looked confused.

"Officer, I don't think these two are like us." T.C. said.

"What did they do? Fall from the sky?"

"Yes, you could say that. I was driving along there was a flash, and they were in front of me."

"I've got a flash for you – what kind of drugs are you taking?" the trooper approached T.C.

Eight of Ten stepped between them. "T.C. is our first contact. You are 376?" he read the numbers on the Trooper's badge.

"That's my number. What kind of a scam are you guys trying to pull?"

"You have reached bandwidth. You are Gods!" they both said.

The other trooper approached the group. "Larry, I've got the governor on the phone. He's been watching this on CNN and he wants us to bring these guys to him. He thinks this might be for real."

"Just wonderful! You, T.C., Get these two into the squad car, and follow us."

"The Borg will go with T.C." Three of Nine said.

"Just what is it you two want?" T.C. asked as they reached his car.

"We are first contact. You have reached bandwidth. You are Gods!" Three of Nine said.

"We will add our biological and technological distinctiveness to you. Our culture will adapt to service yours. We will be enslaved to you." Eight of Ten added.

"Sweet" T.C. smiled.

www: Chapter – 2 – You asked for it!

"...I want to be assimilated. I want to be Borg. Machines will not destroy humans; humans and machine will become one..." Crist Clark

The governor paced the floor. "I'm up for re-election in six months and you people bring some science fiction nuts into my office." He said as he leaned on the wall.

"Governor Johnson, by all accounts these are not some random jokesters. They appear to be Borg." Jessica Llewellyn, the governor's press secretary seemed to be honest in her presentation.

"Dammit! Jessica, you're too young to remember, but there was a popular TV program called *Star Trek* that had all kinds of stories about a so-called Borg species." Governor

Raynor J. Johnson sat behind his desk and gazed at the assembled crowd in his office.

"Oh my God, if this isn't some kind of cruel joke. Who are you people? No, don't tell me, there has to be a Professor in the crowd, some sort of Doctor, a Security person, hangers on...I need a drink!." He placed his head in his hands.

"Excuse me, governor, but I am an Extraterrestrial Anthropologist, and I find this a unique opportunity to reach out to a new race of beings." A short man in a brown suit had pushed his way to the front.

"Doctor Ezra Cloud, Northern University". He extended his hand to the governor.

"Of course you do. And now, you're going to tell us something about the Borg", the governor growled.

"Well, the Borg has a singular goal, namely the consumption of technology, rather than wealth or political expansion as most species seek..." Doctor Cloud began.

"Oh shut-up you idiot! I watched TV as a kid."

The door to the office swung open and T.C. Web walked in, followed by the Borg and the State Troopers. The crowd split to both sides of the room. A horde of reporters and cameramen were trapped in the doorway.

"Gentlemen, ladies, please; we will have one live feed!" Jessica shouted. A CNN camera crew pushed into the center of the room.

T.C. Web stood uneasily before the governor. "Hey, I know you," T.C. said"; You're the guy I didn't vote for!"

"Jessica! Do we need this kind of behavior?" the governor asked.

Jessica Llewellyn took T.C. by the arm. "Please, Mr. Web, restrict your comments to the matters at hand."

"OK, OK. Mr. Governor, the Borg", T.C. said with a sweep of his hand. The Borg stepped front. "This one is Eight of Ten, and this one is Three of Nine."

The governor came around the desk and extended his hand. "It is a pleasure to meet both of you", he said.

"We are Borg. You have reached bandwidth. You are Gods!" they both said.

"Yes, of course we are".

"...This is a Channel 72 news update! I am Kathy Coma reporting live from the governor's office, where, apparently members of the 'Borg' have contacted a Mr. Terrance Commodious Web, also known as T.C. Web, with the request to meet with officials of the State. Apparently, these representatives feel the people of Earth are 'Gods' of some kind..."

"Kathy this is Josh; back at the station. What do we know about these Borg other than what we have seen in popular television shows and the movies?"

"...According to their representatives, the Borg only want to 'raise the quality of life' of any species, they 'assimilate.' Born humanoid, they are almost immediately implanted with biochips that link their brains to a collective consciousness via a unique subspace frequency emitted by each drone. Somehow, someway, they feel the human race has progressed beyond their technology and we can, in fact, benefit them..."

"Kathy, this is Josh again. You spoke of a 'collective consciousness'. Any idea how that maps into the human race?"

"...Josh, all we know is this so-called collective consciousness is experienced by the Borg as 'thousands' of voices — they are collectively aware, but not aware of themselves as separate individuals. Consequently, they never speak in singular pronouns, referring to themselves when required as merely 'Third of Five', for instance..."

"Kathy, is there any way for us to understand any of this?"

"...Josh, I have with me Doctor Ezra Cloud, Northern University an Extraterrestrial Anthropologist. Doctor Cloud can you tell us what is the purpose of this first contact?..."

Doctor Cloud stared into the camera, he seemed uneasy about what he had to say despite his years of facing critics and the public.

"I want to say that after listening to some of the things the Borg have said; I understand what is going on, and I am not certain if mankind should be afraid or rejoicing. Communication is central to borganization. By definition the units making up a borganism will be in close mental contact;

the bandwidth and structure of this contact will determine much of the properties of the borganism. The people of earth have achieved a 'cultural' bandwidth based on the internet, wireless, Bluetooth, cell phone, cable and satellite connections, GPS and a myriad of other integrated technologies, which can keep us in constant contact with the world around us. The Borg achieve this with implants into a human body. To them we are Gods because we *choose* to be 'connected' without implants, and each of us has a level of sophistication based on personal choice, yet we are *ALL* able to be interconnected to each other in some way." Doctor Cloud paused to let the words seep in.

"...So, what are they offering us? In your opinion Doctor Cloud what will we gain from this?..."

"We could gain their technology. They however, see it another way, they see our life as freedom from the collective by personal choice". Doctor Cloud said somberly.

"Doctor Cloud, this is Josh, back at the station. This sounds like an opportunity for mankind to reach out to an alien species and return its humanity".

"Perhaps Josh. Or perhaps there will be humans who crave more connectivity, more communications with each other, and chose to become Borg, themselves".

"...So, there you have it in a nutshell, a chance to change things. This is Kathy Coma, WKYW Channel 72 at the governor's office, with the Borg. Back to you Josh!..."

"Is that it? Is that what you're going to leave the world thinking about?" Doctor Cloud said as he pulled on the newscasters' arm.

"Hey, Doc, get a grip. I have to cover a story about a midget hooker who sleeps with a Bunyip". Kathy Coma pushed her way through the crowd and towards the door.

www: Chapter – the last

The case was not as clear for voluntary borganisms where units both retain a sense of individuality and still belong to the borganism. Some wanted to stay Borg, some wanted to join us, in the end...

...*Resistance was futile.*[15]

---

[15] I want to thank:
Speculations on Hive Minds as a Post Human State by Anders Sandberg; http://www.aleph.se/Trans/Global/Posthumanity/WeBorg.html, for planting the seeds to this story.

Obituary:
Rambo (The Cat) Bisol

Rambo, beloved pet of the Bisol family for almost two decades, passed away yesterday after a lengthy illness. Rambo left two associates, Mr. Moon and Buffalo Bob Bisol. He was predeceased by his Stepsister Lilly.

Rambo was an original "Docktor Pet" cat. He was gentle in nature and had a fondness for anything organic he thought he could eat. Rambo survived a "Thread-ectomy" procedure after eating a quantity of sewing thread. (He was Liposuctioned at the same time). More recently, Rambo had undergone two major surgeries for cancer and a tumor on his paw. Throughout all his mishaps, Rambo maintained an even humor and spent most of his time lolling on the couch and snoring in the sunlight.

Despite his even demeanor, Rambo abandoned his Stepsister Lily in favor of a Younger "Chickee", Mr. Moon several years ago. Lately Rambo had no tolerance for Mr. Moon and frequently spat at her. It was apparent that he was suffering from remorse for his previous sins.

When asked for a comment, Buffalo Bob (Generally a clueless, sometimes forlorn, cat), could only remark, "There's something missing next to the wood stove". (An obvious reference to Rambo's private convalescence room, complete with food, water, and kitty litter.)

For a long time, Mr. Moon simply sat in the space once occupied by Rambo, staring off into space (as cats often do). By the next day, it appears she had regained her "schizoid" attitude and was once again jitter jumping at the approach of a human.

Rambo could best be remembered for his ability to "suck-in" his body and face, to appear gaunt when he begged for food scraps. He had no shame and would track crumbs from across the room. As a point of fact, he would eat rubber bands as witnessed by a veterinarian mandated stool sample. Although not noted for his athletic prowess, Rambo could, in his younger days, leap from the floor to the high windowsill in a single bound. He was a "closet" coward, having run from a raccoon that appeared at the cellar door one evening – hiding for two days afterwards.

Rambo will be sorely missed by the family, but informed sources have said "all the issues have been resolved", and "what do you want me to say, he was old!"

Happy Hunting - Rambo, rest in peace.

The Third Book of Moses: Called Leviticus -Chapter 20

20:1 And the LORD spoke unto Moses, saying,

20:2 Again, thou shall say to the children of Israel, Whosoever he is of the children of Israel, or of the strangers that sojourn in Israel, that gives any of his seed unto Molech; he shall surely be put to death: the people of the land shall stone him with stones.

20:3 And I will set my face against that man, and will cut him off from among his people; because he hath given of his seed unto Molech, to defile my sanctuary, and to profane my holy name.

20:4 And if the people of the land do any ways hide their eyes from the man, when he gives of his seed unto Molech, and kill him not:

20:5 Then I will set my face against that man, and against his family, and will cut him off, and all that go a whoring after him, to commit whoredom with Molech, from among their people.

20:6 And the soul that turned after such as have familiar spirits, and after wizards, to go a whoring after them, I will even set my face against that soul, and will cut him off from among his people.

20:7 Sanctify yourselves therefore, and be ye holy: for I am the LORD your God.

20:8 And ye shall keep my statutes, and do them: I am the LORD which sanctify you.

20:9 For every one that curses his father or his mother shall be surely put to death: he hath cursed his father or his mother; his blood shall be upon him.

20:10 And the man that commits adultery with another man's wife, even he that commits adultery with his neighbor's wife, the adulterer and the adulteress shall surely be put to death.

20:11 And the man that lies with his father's wife hath uncovered his father's nakedness: both of them shall surely be put to death; their blood shall be upon them.

20:12 And if a man lie with his daughter in law, both of them shall surely be put to death: they have wrought confusion; their blood shall be upon them.

20:13 If a man also lie with mankind, as he lies with a woman, both of them have committed an abomination: they shall surely be put to death; their blood shall be upon them.

20:14 And if a man take a wife and her mother, it is wickedness: they shall be burnt with fire, both he and they; that there be no wickedness among you.

20:15 And if a man lie with a beast, he shall surely be put to death: and ye shall slay the beast.

20:16 And if a woman approach unto any beast, and lie down thereto, thou shall kill the woman, and the beast: they shall surely be put to death; their blood shall be upon them.

20:17 And if a man shall take his sister, his father's daughter, or his mother's daughter, and see her nakedness and she see his nakedness; it is a wicked thing; and they shall be cut off in the sight of their people: he hath uncovered his sister's nakedness; he shall bear his iniquity.

20:18 And if a man shall lie with a woman having her sickness, and shall uncover her nakedness; he hath discovered her fountain, and she hath uncovered the fountain of her blood: and both of them shall be cut off from among their people.

20:19 And thou shall not uncover the nakedness of thy mother's sister, nor of thy father's sister: for he uncovered his near kin: they shall bear their iniquity.

20:20 And if a man shall lie with his uncle's wife, he hath uncovered his uncle's nakedness: they shall bear their sin; they shall die childless.

20:21 And if a man shall take his brother's wife, it is an unclean thing: he hath uncovered his brother's nakedness; they shall be childless.

20:22 Ye shall therefore keep all my statutes, and all my judgments, and do them: that the land, whither I bring you to dwell therein, spew you not out.

20:23 And ye shall not walk in the manners of the nation, which I cast out before you: for they committed all these things, and therefore I abhorred them.

20:24 But I have said unto you, Ye shall inherit their land, and I will give it unto you to possess it, a land that flowed with milk and honey: I am the LORD your God, which have separated you from other people.

20:25 Ye shall therefore put difference between clean beasts and unclean, and between unclean fowls and clean: and ye shall not make your souls abominable by beast, or by fowl, or by any manner of living thing that creeps on the ground, which I have separated from you as unclean.

20:26 And ye shall be holy unto me: for I the LORD am holy, and have severed you from other people, that ye should be mine.

20:27 A man also or woman that hath a familiar spirit, or that is a wizard, shall surely be put to death: they shall stone them with stones: their blood shall be upon them.

"...Just in case you forgot what you should or should not be doing with your spare time..." AUTHOR

<u>CSI - AUTOPSY REPORT – FINAL</u>

Date: Thursday, October 19, 2006

Subjects: Three Gold Fish: a.k.a. Carpet; Paws; Misfit

Age: 4+ years

Location: 10-Gallon Tank   Hudson, Ma 01749-1131

Subject fish died on or about October 9th, 2006. Found as "floaters" belly up or on-end in tank. Investigation revealed that the subjects had been "nipping" and "biting" the decorative sandstone lighthouse in the tank. Large portions of the finish of the lighthouse had been removed on the "hidden" side. It was well known that the three subjects spent most of their time ingesting and spitting out the aquarium stones at the bottom of the tank. This behavior was believed to an "algae cleansing action". Maybe, but the lighthouse was made of beach sand and there is no doubt that the ingestion of large quantities of sand, paint chips, and silica products is not good for anyone. The subjects were unable to process this sand as "food" and died either of constipation or of just being weighted down. In the future, this will be a "one fish" tank – without adornment.

"FINITO"